Sir Conman

By Jonathan M Wiggins

New Generation Publishing

Chapter 1

It all began in Doncaster. It's 1987, I was seven years old, my birthday being the 2nd May 1980. My mother, Jane, my father, Richard, my older brother by three years Robert and myself all live in a scruffy, old, three-bedroom council house.

My father worked as a forklift truck driver at a big packaging factory on the other side of town. He already had plans for Robert and me to join him. I can still hear him say "If it's good enough for me it's good enough for you!" Somehow, I don't think so! I was aware that he had a lot of debts. We never went on holiday; the house was like an empty shell and the carpets were threadbare. My mother always did her best as a stay at home mum, even though it was a miserable kind of existence. If my father wasn't at work then he was fishing or messing around with an old mini that he kept in the garage with his oh so great friend Gary- Mr Know It All!

Other than school I would spend most of my time in my room. Robert and I never got on and just stayed away from each other. I didn't have any friends. No invites to parties, that was when I knew that I was different. For some reason I just couldn't bond with other children. Don't get me wrong I can never recall feeling lonely, I just didn't like other people very much. My looks never really did me any favours. I was average height, skinny and gaunt with wavy brown hair. Oh, and I was never tidy. I once overheard my father describing me as the runt of the litter. That I have never forgotten! I wanted better than this, some people will settle for nothing and I'm not one of those people. The person I felt sorry for the most was my mother. She did her best, but my father had made her believe that it was fine to have nothing!

School, Coalsville Primary, was only a five-minute walk away from our house. I really enjoyed being there as the teachers were nice. I got on quite well, but I still didn't have any friends. I got teased and pushed around by the other children, but it wasn't any major problem. By this point I had just accepted that I am who I am. The next school, Sir William George Secondary, was on the other side of town. To a twelve-year-old this place is bloody enormous, I absolutely hated every second. I would do almost anything not to go but sometimes it was easier to go than trying to get out of it. The only good thing that came out of that fucking horrible place was that I made a friend, Kevin. We were genuinely cut from the same cloth. Both council house kids, poor and with nothing to hope for in the future. We were almost inseparable, he'd stay at my house and I'd stay at his.

When my brother left he went straight to the factory to work with my father. I could see that he hated it but it kept father happy. Kevin went to scouts every Wednesday evening and kept on at me to join, but I really wasn't interested at all. But then my mother and father started telling me to join. "Go on it will be good for you, who knows you might even enjoy it!" so I finally gave in, more to shut them up than anything else. I'm looking forward to going on a camping trip to Hereford in five weeks' time. It's only three nights, but all the same it is still away from here, or so I thought. All packed up and ready to go, there must have been 20 of us and the 3 leaders: Mr Lewis, Mr Robins and Mr Thomas. We were in a big field on a farm in the middle of nowhere. The first thing we had to do was erect the tents and build a couple of camp fires. The three older boys had to pick who they wanted in their tents, I was the last one left, and nobody wanted me. So, Mr Robins said "You'll have to come in with me" I remember it like it was yesterday. It was getting late and I really didn't like this. He had a two-man tent, I really didn't like this. I even asked if I could sleep in the mini bus, but the answer was point blank no. He unzipped the tent and I went in first and chose the sleeping bag on the left. He told me to get undressed, I took my vest off but kept my shorts on.

The camp was silent. I rolled onto my side with my back to him and fell asleep. The next thing I know I wake up, he is kneeling by my side completely naked. His right hand is around my throat and his left hand is forcing its way into my shorts. I'm scared witless! The ordeal must have lasted half an hour I had nowhere to run, I was trapped. When he'd finished I was told to keep my mouth shut and that it never happened. The following day I tried my hardest to swap with anyone but to no avail I knew what was coming that night and I wasn't wrong.

He was a school governor and a local business man. He was very well respected by everyone, I know for a fact no one would believe me over him. The final blow was yet to come on the last day. All the other boys had abandoned me and were down by the river, so I grabbed a bin bag and went litter picking just to stay away from him. I looked round to see him and Mr Lewis walking towards me. Relief at last, Mr Lewis was here. "Adam can you give us a quick hand taking down a rope swing?" I agreed and the three of us walked into the woods. As we entered a heavily wooded area I thought I hadn't seen a rope swing here. I was thrown to the floor and they took turns to rape me. Mr Lewis took photographs and informed me that if I said one word I would end up at the bottom of the river and that no one would believe me!

All the way home I was kicked and punched, and I cannot express my relief of when I saw my dad waiting for me. Mr Lewis walked over with me and explained what a wonderful time we had all had. I was covered in bruises and scuffs. I didn't return after that and to this day I still hold Kevin partly responsible. What a truly awful experience! I've since learnt that Mr Lewis is dead, and I don't know about Mr Robins but hopefully he's rotting in a prison cell somewhere!

Seven months later my father was crushed to death by falling pallets. It was a total shock to everyone as he was only forty-four. After a lengthy enquiry, the verdict was accidental. My mother received minimal compensation. I think she paid off some debts and then all the money was gone. My father was dead, my brother was in Liverpool living with his girlfriend Claire and Mr Know It All- Gary- had moved in. God only knows what my mother sees in him, genuinely he was a total dickhead. Robert had the right idea, getting out when he did. I've only seen him once and it looks like he's doing well. They've both got jobs and their own flat, so good luck to them. I just can't get on with Gary. He's rude, arrogant and full of shit. I know what his plan is; get rid of me as soon as possible then the two of them can live happily ever after. My mother's getting as bad as him! Taking his side and backing him up all the time.

Chapter 2

It's 1998, I'm eighteen and have left school with very average exam results. I keep applying for jobs, but the truth is, I really haven't got a clue what I want to do. Most evenings I would either sit alone in my room or be in the Butchers Arms, our local pub.

Gary informed me that his mate is a supervisor at a local supermarket and that they're looking for people to work in the warehouse. I really didn't want to do this job but as usual I was pressured into it. But on the other hand, this was my chance to finally make some friends. I got offered the job on a Thursday and agreed to start the following Monday. The pay was minimum wage but all the bullshit about how I could become a manager in two years followed. This job brings a new meaning to mind numbing. Just tedious and boring! After a couple weeks I struck up a friendship with a guy called Pete. He was a local guy who had worked there a couple years. It's beyond me how anyone could stick at this for that long. All the same at least I had someone to sit in the pub with at night.

The tension at home was getting worse with all the constant arguing, I'd just about had enough. Pete offered me a room at his house, his parents agreed and off I went. The evening I left I could tell by my mother's face that she was doing exactly as she was told and Mr Know It All didn't even say goodbye. Up to this day I don't know why she let him play her like a fiddle.

I had been at Pete's about five months. It was pleasant, but I just didn't feel I belonged there. Summing it up, I had a job I hated, I was living with people that didn't really want me around and didn't have a penny to my name. Something had to change, I wasn't sure what or how, with no money and very little going for me.

I contacted my Aunt Ruby, she lives near Marble Arch in London. Aunt Ruby lived alone in a massive house, her and my uncle had split up years ago. Aunt Ruby said I was more than welcome. There was no time to waste.

I knew Pete's mum had money in a tin hidden in the wardrobe. It was just over £600.00. It will have to do. It's enough to get me out of here. I phoned in sick. Packed two holdalls, that was all I had to show for eighteen years, grabbed the cash and went off to the station.

I had to wait around an hour for the train. I'm happy to be leaving here, but also sad that nothing went my way. Looking out of the train window, I'm thinking how easy it was to steal the cash and run. Perhaps I could be onto something here.

Aunt Ruby is waiting at the platform, I can just see her, she hasn't changed much. Looks a bit like a retired hippy who tried to smarten herself up. But thank god, she was my only lifeline. We arrive at her house, a four-story town house, very impressive. Six bedrooms, three bathrooms, a far cry from what I was used to.

I've only got just over £500.00 left and know it won't last long here. I will have to put my thinking cap on. Aunt Ruby works mornings at an art gallery. I try to find out as much information about my Uncle. After about a week I think I have got everything I need.

I apply for 8 credit cards in his name, all I have to do is sit and wait, oh and make sure I pick up the post. After a while I am accepted on all of the cards. I had a total limit of nearly forty thousand pounds, with the name of Sir Adam Robert Cleaver, on each card. Brilliant, free money. I wanted the lifestyle, Champagne, coke, Bentleys and why not after the shit life I have had.

As time went on I was introduced to some of Aunt Ruby's friends, usually at dinner parties. One person I hit it off with straight away was Gwen a retired Antiques Dealer. Gwen was single, a millionaire and lives near Harley Street. It was strange, I was 18 and Gwen was 51. She took me to expensive restaurants, posh events and members only clubs. I was like a little brother to her. Gwen bought me jewellery, watches, clothes, anything I wanted I got it. All I had to do was sleep with her.

Around eight weeks later Gwen invited me to move in. I jumped at the chance. By now I am as good as skint. I've maxed out on the cards. As far as I knew Aunt Ruby still doesn't know about these. Aunt Ruby didn't approve of us, but I didn't care.

When Gwen and I go out I'm now known as Sir Adam, Gwen thought this was a good idea. When you have a title, people treat you with respect. Plus, usually they will bend over backwards for you. I have noticed that Gwen has quite a heavy drink and drugs problem. I'm not bothered, I'm only here for a free ride. Two choices I suppose live it up here or return to the misery of Doncaster. Well it's a no brainer.

Then one Saturday night it all came crashing down. Gwen and I had been out for a meal followed by some bars. We were hammered and arrived back at the house just before 3am. Gwen paid the cab and I went in first, Gwen was only a few steps behind me. I heard a thudding crash and saw Gwen on the floor, she was shaking all over, I couldn't wake her. An Ambulance arrived, and we were taken to St George's Hospital. The Paramedic thinks she may have suffered a stroke. By 7 o'clock a doctor tells me Gwen has had a brain haemorrhage and they didn't expect her to last the next 48 hours.

This sounds awful, what am I going to do, I was panicking, is this the end of the free ride. As we weren't married I was entitled to nothing. Just after lunch time I returned to the house to freshen up, but more than anything to stash away anything of value, most of which was rings, watches, necklaces. I also had her handbag containing cash and cards. I knew all the pin numbers for her cards. How selfish and greedy am I. However, I had to look out for number one.

Gwen lasted 3 more days before she passed away. Just myself and Aunt Ruby were at her bedside. Now I am on my own and getting very anxious about what lay ahead. The only thing I am good at is lying, cheating and stealing. I have no choice but to continue.

The next eight to ten days are a complete blur. I drank bottle after bottle and put away enough coke to kill a horse. Money was running out fast. I owed a drug dealer eighteen hundred and a Limousine Company thirteen hundred. I'm selling off anything I can and spending it even faster.

It is early on a Tuesday morning and the phone rings. I'm in a shocking state and pissed. I answer the phone and its Aunt Ruby politely informing me that Gwen's daughter is flying in from Canada on Thursday. Gwen never mentioned a daughter, now this really isn't good news for me. I have virtually stripped the place, sold off almost everything and she will also want me out. I can't think straight, what the hell am I going to do. I'm used to getting my own way, somehow, I think not this time. Oh! and to top it all Aunt Ruby informs me that debt collectors are looking for me regarding certain credit cards. All I have left is some posh clothes, a posh accent and a made-up title, things were crashing fast.

Gwen's daughter and husband Paul arrive on Thursday afternoon. The first thing she says is

Gwen's funeral is next Friday, this really doesn't matter as I won't be going and where the hell is everything? I explained that her Mother had sold everything to support her habit. I think she knew it was me, there wasn't even a picture left hanging on the wall, anything of value was gone, the place was not far off a squat. She in no uncertain terms reveals that if I leave before next Friday she will give me £1000 in cash. I know I had no option other than to accept her offer.

Within the week I was packed and ready to go. She kept her word handing me my £1000 and the last thing I said to her I will see you at the funeral, I have no intention of going. Gwen was just a free ride and it was a good time whilst it lasted.

Leaving here now I have got to be very careful. I have got Debt Collectors, Dealers and a Limo Company, all looking for me. One thing if you look posh, sound posh and behave in a certain manner, people want to be with you. Perhaps I will have to play on this now. I wouldn't go back to Aunt Ruby's, I think she is a bit pissed off with me and Doncaster is a definite none starter.

Chapter 3

So, armed with two holdalls and £1000 in cash I get a cab to the George Cross Pub in Kings Cross. This is how sly I am, taking my holdalls I tell the cab driver to wait, he must have thought this geezer is good for a few quid. I walk straight through the pub and out of the back door. I think the fare was £18.60, god how my looks cloud people. I just love drinking Champagne, snorting coke and living it up, all at someone else's expense. If they are giving it away I will take it and more. You know I didn't even feel an ounce of shame or guilt. As long as I am alright I couldn't give a toss. Once I had escaped through the pub I walked half a mile to the Red Lion, where I enjoyed a large Gin and Tonic and for once paid in cash. That was a very odd feeling, I am a Sir and given freebee's, how dare I actually pay for something. This is the point where I do believe it all went totally out of control. I'm going to fleece and con wherever I can.

That night I found myself staying in a low-class budget hotel called Owls house in Charring Cross. It was £90 a night, a real drop down from what I had become used to. It is a bit damp and grubby but I suppose it will have to do for now.

My next target will be Charles, a top London Barrister and close friend of Aunt Ruby. I met him at my Aunts dinner parties. Charles is a tall man, in his late 50's, married with three grown up children, he lives in Chiswick and drives a new Jaguar. I also know he is as bent as they come and a big coke head. The last time I saw him he gave me his number in case I needed him. Oh! This was just before he touched by bottom when we were in my Aunts study, yes! he will do nicely. I call him and arrange to meet for a drink that night in the Golden Globe Hotel in Hammersmith. Charles is well up for it, we arrange to meet at 7.30pm. I arrive at 7pm, more than anything to check out the place. Yes! There is plenty of money kicking around here. I take the corner seat and sip my gin and tonic, quality place, quality people and huge amounts parked outside. Yes perfect.

Charles arrives at 7.30pm, "how can I help you" Charles says, no there is nothing I just thought it would be nice to have a drink and a chat, I haven't seen you for a while. We sit and talk, he buys all of the drinks. Just as well it is a bit pricey in here. I know what is really on his mind, I'm making him wait.

It's just before 11 o'clock and Charles asks if I would like to carry on our meeting upstairs with some coke and a bottle of Dom Perignon, he has fallen hook line and sinker into my trap. We have been in the room about twenty minutes and Charles enters the bathroom. I take the opportunity to prop my phone on the dressing table and press record. Charles is totally unaware that he is going to be blackmailed, he even snorted coke off me. Hopefully I have got everything I need. In one way I enjoyed it knowing I had him just where I wanted him.

The next morning Charles leaves the hotel around 7.45am. Before he departs he leaves me some coke and two hundred pounds. Now alone I grab my phone and check out the footage, it's perfect, every sordid moment. Twenty thousand pounds is my asking price with no room for negotiation. I am not proud of myself but needs must. I know he has got plenty of cash and I need some. I rang him at lunch time and said in 10 minutes I will send you a video, I want twenty thousand pounds in cash. I will be under the bridge next to Baker Street Station, just up from Zeds Café, at midday on Friday. I could absolutely ruin him, I don't want to I just want the cash.

Charles arrives on time, passes me a bundle and I give my word our business will go no further and we go our separate ways. Anyone who has crossed paths with me will tell you my word means absolutely fuck all. I am a nasty little shit putting it politely.

Chapter 4

I have decided to stay in the hotel for another week. I suppose it will do for now as I am in town all day I only need a roof over my head. I am getting my own web page, so people can see who I am, this is all made up crap, a photo of me standing next to a brand new Rolls Royce, another standing outside a mansion in Oxfordshire. It states my net worth is £100 million pounds and a made-up family of Lords and Ladies. This is £900 very well spent,

I have paid off my first dealer, he was getting slightly heavy to say the least, but I still owe two more. My habit is escalating very fast. I only drink Champagne or Gin and Tonic, I'm pissed and high every day now. Also spending like there is no tomorrow, £240.00 on a jacket, £250.00 on shoes, a £100.00 on designer aftershave and oh the cravat of course, just to finish off the look.

I am now in a more upmarket hotel closer to town, a fourposter bed, room service, my laundry is done and they even clean my shoes when I want. I do wonder about my Mother and Brother, I can't contact them, I have to stay lost in the crowd, I have got too many people after me to reveal my whereabouts. I didn't want to end up beaten to a pulp or inside. I am actually enjoying myself for once.

Whilst being here I have made a contact, Jimmy one of those people who can get you anything. I have now got a cheque book in the name of Sir Adam Robert Cleaver, on it also £500 worth of counterfeit notes for £250.00, money well spent. I made sure I didn't go to the same place more than twice. I owe two more Limo Companies now, I have no intention of paying them, I guess I will just have to watch my back.

Another nice little trick of mine is when sitting in a group of people having an expensive dinner and Champagne, only in a Michelin star restaurant of course, near the end of the dinner go to the bathroom, phone my driver and demand to meet him around the corner in exactly 15 minutes. When he is there he will call me, I will then explain, very sorry Ladies and Gentlemen, I have to take this it's my office in Australia, please excuse me. With the phone at my ear I walk outside, into the car and disappear into the night. A nice little touch to round off the day. Its not my fault people wanted to be with me.

I have now been in London just under 3 years. I am looking now at another style of Con. I obtain 50 Rohypnol tablets from Jimmy, I arrive at The Dorchester and sit alone at the bar, I know there are very rich gay business men that congregate here most evenings. Very smartly dressed, looking good, I take a corner seat with a Gin and Tonic in hand. After an hour or so a very well dressed stocky man, maybe late 50's, politely asks if this seat is taken, "no sir help yourself", he removes his jacket, shakes my hand and introduces himself as Lawrence. Lawrence buys me another Gin and Tonic, I introduce myself as Sir Adam. Lawrence is a property tycoon and staying here for two nights, I reveal I am waiting for a friend, not really just another lie.

Lawrence's usual mode of transport is a helicopter, it is very obvious straight away he is loaded. I am trying to keep the conversation more about him than me, the less he knows about me the better. Straight to my attention is a huge chunky gold watch, I am sure it is a Rolex, gold rings and a nice gold bracelet, I am not sure what is in his wallet though. It is getting near 11pm, the bar is slowly emptying, he hasn't made a move on me yet, so I force his hand. Saying very nice to meet you Lawrence but I must go now, as I reach for my jacket he places his hand on my wrist and very quietly asks if I would like to stay the night. Bingo got him.

Things could still go wrong and so I am still a little nervous. We entre his room, well it is more like a luxury apartment. Lawrence orders a bottle of Champagne and two large malt whiskeys. Lawrence tips the waiter with a twenty and locks the door. I take off my jacket and put some music on. Lawrence looks over his shoulder and say's to my surprise, do you have any protection with you? I am a bit shocked, I hadn't thought of it. Don't worry I will go and get some, I will be back in 5 minutes. This was enough time to pour and drug his drink, Champagne poured I slipped 3 Rohypnol into his drink. On Lawrence's return we just sat and chatted, finished the bottle and by 1.30am he was spark out cold, Lawrence was breathing but totally unconscious. Within minutes I had searched his room and taken anything and everything of any value, his watch, jewellery and £920 in cash. After tidying myself up, I washed the glasses thoroughly. I must have bagged six or seven grand at least, maybe more. I did say sorry as I left, I know he couldn't hear me. Lawrence was actually a really nice guy, just unlucky that he came across me. As the man opened the door I slipped him one of my dodgy £20 notes and said thank you. Poor old Lawrence couldn't exactly go home and tell his wife he has been ripped off by a two-bit rent boy or even worse, go to the Police.

I pulled this off time and time again, always having the sense to change my appearance, hair style, sometimes a beard, glasses. It worked perfect every time. I have done this 10 maybe 11 times, still feeling no guilt or shame, I realise I have become a posh upmarket rent boy. Women have been doing this for years and got away with it, the only difference is I take a bit more than perhaps I should.

My number one con was Chester House Hotel Park Lane, arriving with Chauffer driven Bentley, dressed to perfection even wearing Gucci aftershave. Into the bar I went, this time I am approached by an American gentleman introducing himself as Hudson a Shipping

Tycoon from Boston. Age wise Hudson was probably about 61 maybe 62, again a very nice generous man. I stuck to the same routine, this time jewellery, cash and cards, it was over thirty thousand. Most of this I will off load to pawn shops, there are so many to choose from.

I am rolling in cash, the best of everything for me, my dealers are all paid off too. I haven't paid any of the Limo Companies, I know they were overcharging me to start with. With over sixty thousand stashed I am going to ground for a while. I have wanted to do something about my complexion for some time, I use makeup to hide it, it has mainly been caused by coke and booze. I am off to see a surgeon at Harley Street called Dr Cason, my list consists of having my nose straightened, bags removed from under my eyes and wrinkles smoothed away, the total cost is £9000. I agree I will be in his clinic for two days, then two maybe three weeks after to recover. One week later it's all systems go, the surgery is a success, but I need to rest now. I spent a couple of weeks in my hotel room watching television, reading, drinking way too much Champagne. But managed to keep off the coke. Just my room service alone came to over £1200 for the two weeks. Once the two weeks had passed I return to see Dr Cason. He's very pleased and all is healing nicely. I must admit I do look much better.

Chapter 5

One evening sitting in the bar I read of a charity auction being held at the Grosvenor on Saturday night. Its founder is Lady Penelope Christopher Hughes and it is in aid of a children's cancer charity. This is like a red rag to a bull. I've been off the scene a few weeks, I needed a buzz. A completely different style of con. I'm questioning myself, am I up to it? Is it too risky? No, I'll go for it! Who would dare question me I'm a sir!

So a chauffeur driven Mercedes collects me from a bar half a mile from my hotel. Can't have anyone knowing where I'm staying. I arrive at 7:45, the auction starts at 8:30. It's very posh in here and very hot I am starting to sweat. I am greeted by a lovely lady I now know to be Lady Penelope, she greets me with open arms." Oh! so wonderful to see you, do have a lovely evening". Little does she know what my true intentions are. It is all ball gowns and dinner jackets here. My wallet contains reals of fake cards, a worthless cheque book from an exclusive London Bank and about £500 in cash, some of that is not real either. I mingle with a few people informing them I am a millionaire property developer based in Paris and Canada, but only in London for three days on business. No one had any reason to doubt me. My eyes are all over the room, almost scanning, to see if I recognise anybody, but I am sure the coast is clear.

As the auction begins I realise only small objects are for me. A six-foot oil painting is no good. The smaller the better, easy to transport and sell on. The first half interval approaches, this gives me time to suss out what is left. Two items stand out, a bronze of a race horse and a gorgeous diamond and ruby necklace set in white gold. Yes, these will do nicely. The horse is lot 31 and the necklace is lot 44. First up is the horse, it is very popular at least 13 to 15 people were bidding, it reached £12,200 and the bidding stalled. I threw my hand in the air £13,000 and the hammer fell with a massive round of applause.

Time for a quick line and another Gin and Tonic. One chap on our table asks, "anything else taken your fancy?" "No, I am not sure yet, "I say. Twenty minutes later the necklace arrives, what a beautiful piece. The atmosphere is tense, the bidding starts at £5,000 and is going up £1,000 at a time. It slowed down to £28,000, went in at £29,000 then £30,000. The auctioneer is asking £31,000, the room falls silent, I shout out £31,000. Going once, going twice, sold. Yet again a huge round of applause. Now I just want to run but I had to hang on until the end.

I had another line in the bathroom and called Terry, the guy who dropped me off, demand he be outside bang on 12.30am. All I had to do was stay calm and hold myself together. At exactly

12.20am I find Lady Penelope and present her with a cheque for £50,000. Before she could speak I said use the extra which ever way you feel. Thank you, she beamed with delight and gratitude. I don't know what to say, thank you so much, this will go an awfully long way. Showing me a side room to collect my articles, I put the necklace in my inside pocket and carried the horse. All together it is about the size of a shoe box, it did weigh a bit.

I made my way to the exit, one hand covering part of my face to avoid any cameras. I can see Terry waiting through the glass. Six feet from the door a voice comes from behind, excuse me sir, I just froze on the spot, shit. I turned starting to sweat, I cannot run I'm busted. Would you like any packaging? No thank you. I rush to the car and we are gone.

Terry dropped me off where he picked me up. It's 1.15am and a short walk to my hotel. I am in total heaven, what a great scam. Within a week all she had got is a worthless piece of paper. What a cruel bastard I am. Room service delivers a bottle of Champagne and I admire my evenings work. I am over the moon, how low ripping off a child's charity, but it is done now. I will see what I can get for them in the next day or two. How have I resorted to this? All I conclude is I grew up with nothing, literally nothing.

I may leave here tomorrow and head off to Surrey, there is high end pawn shops there. I will keep the horse for now, I still have a Rolex and a couple of rings, plus the necklace to get rid of.

The next morning, I shave off my beard and dress as a country gent, pack my belongings and check out. I won't be using Terry anymore, I must owe him £300.00. I promised I would pay him today but that is not going to happen. When checking out I leave the staff £200.00 as a tip, to share between them, see I am not so bad after all. Armed with my loot, £70,000 in cash, dodgy credit cards, a dodgy cheque book oh and some rohypnol, I jump into a black cab and Surrey is my next destination.

If I am successful in getting rid of the jewellery I am going up to Scotland. I feel like I am pushing my luck. I arrive in Weybridge, it is just after lunch time. I am in an internet Café, coffee and search for a Country House Hotel near to Glasgow. I've found one, The Angus Glen, a 5star hotel. It is £180 per night and there is a train that leaves at 4.15pm. I phone and book for one week. Informing them that I may not arrive until late, the train gets me to Glasgow for 8.20pm, so I should be there at 9pm.

I haven't had any contact with my mother or Robert for some considerable time, I will write her a short note, wishing them well and that I am living and working in Surrey, love always Adam and post it here as to not give away my true whereabouts. I better get a move on my train leaves at 4.15 pm and its now 2pm, but I am only a 5-minute walk from the station.

I find a pawn brokers, I have a cap and glasses on and try to hide my face as much as possible. I now just want rid of the jewellery and to get up to Scotland. I am greeted by a man called James. How can I help? I have some items I would like to sell, passing them under the window I see his face light up. Do you mind me asking where you acquired these items? Yes, my Aunt left them for me in her will. OK, can you give me an hour to look them over? Yes, of course, I will see you in an hour. The paranoia hits, has he sussed me? Is he calling the Police? There are only two choices either I run or wait, I am going to wait, my nerves are shot.

I find a pub along the road, a large Gin and Tonic and a quick line should square me up. I can see the Pawn shop from the window and there is nothing unusual going on that I can see. Just stay calm, relax. To think I could be in a Police cell within hours. Not if I have my way. I am fixated on the shop, the Barman is giving me some strange looks, I tell him I am waiting for a friend.

Since leaving Doncaster I must have gained two or three stone. It just shows you what the high life does to you. When I worked at the Supermarket I did not touch drugs and drank very little, god now look.

Right an hour has passed and a very long one at that, back to see James. Are the Police waiting for me? It is as if I am playing a game of dare. Back in the shop all looks clear. James says he can offer me £2,600 for the watch, £1,400 for the rings and £7,000 for the necklace, total £11,000. Yes thanks, they were only sitting in a draw. We shake hands and he counts me out £11,000 in cash. Perfect, I am off like a shot. It is not long, and I am off to Glasgow, the only thing I thought may go wrong was he wanted to see some ID. I showed him some bank cards and my cheque book, which he photocopied. I now have just over £80,000 in cash. One thing that would come in very handy is a passport, I will have to look into it.

First class on the train Champagne flowing. I am looking forward to a nice break. I do wonder if the auction was a step too far, but it is done now, it's what I am good at. If you have got the front and can keep your cool I believe you can get away with almost anything.

Whilst in Weybridge I purchased a new laptop and pay as you go phone. My coke supply was running a bit low I will have to find some in Glasgow. This actually feels quite strange, the last time I boarded a train was leaving Doncaster to stay at Aunt Ruby's, I wonder how she is? Does she wonder how I am? It has been over four years since I saw her or my Mother and Robert.

Reminiscing over the last four plus years, how many people have I ripped off, deceived, stolen from and blackmailed, fifty maybe sixty, it could be even more, I honestly don't know. That word honest really doesn't sit well with me for obvious reasons. Do I feel any remorse, sorrow, shame or quilt, no of course not, why should I. If you put yourself to me and leave yourself wide open of course I will take advantage, what do you expect. My Grandfather always taught me to keep my eye's and ears open and my mouth shut, excellent advice.

Chapter 6

I arrive in Glasgow on time, it was a pleasant journey with no hick ups. I take a cab to the hotel, it is about twenty minutes away, in the middle of nowhere. It suits me fine. It is only a couple of weeks until Christmas, I need to rest, and this looks like the perfect place. The drive leading to the Hotel must be a mile long. A magnificent mansion style building, with a golf course to the rear and a lake out front, surrounded by woodland, a perfect hiding place.

For once I pay the cab driver, £26.20, I gave him £30.00. I make my entrance and pay in full for the three weeks. A guy probably around my age, Stuart, takes my bags and shows me to my room. Well it's more like a luxury flat, real quality, separate sitting room, a mini bar, massive bed, plasma television, you name it. I pass Stuart £10.00 and he leaves.

I unpack, it's getting late, I order a bottle of Champagne and Gin and tonic. I shower and settle down for the night. One thing is troubling me, I am nearly out of coke, I will head into Glasgow tomorrow and have a nose about. I put my laptop and phone on charge, it is nearby. It is time to call it a day, I must have just passed out, that was more than nerve racking in Surrey.

It is 9am and I have breakfast in my room, Stuart appears with it, we make small talk and he informs me that the Hotel have their own Limousine service, free of charge within a certain distance. This is really good news, I book to be taken to Glasgow at midday. A big black Mercedes waits for me outside, Graham is my driver," to the City sir?" Yes, thank you. Within 25 minutes we are approaching the city, Graham passes me a card with his number on, to call when I want collecting. I have got £2,000 in cash on me, just thinking I am a bit like Robin Hood instead of taking from the rich and giving to the poor, I just take from the rich and keep it for myself. I have instructed Graham to pick me up at 5 o'clock, by the clock tower.

I wander around for half and hour, trying to find an establishment where I may fit in. I finally settle for a pub restaurant called The Crown and Anchor, it is worth a try I suppose, I have to start somewhere. It is actually very nice in here, not too busy, that's good. A Gin and Tonic and a corner table for me. I enter the lavatory and a guy follows me in. Hi mate haven't seen you in here before. No, I am only here a short time on business. If you need anything I am your man. Actually, there is, come and join me.

I am Adam, well it is actually, Sir Adam. I am Jay, how can I help you? Let's get another drink, I can tell he is not someone you mess about with. Jay must be 6ft 5, tattoos everywhere and must be 20 stone and the leather jacket of course. Can you get me some coke? Yeah, no problem, how much? £700.00, have you got the cash? I open my wallet. Give me an hour he's gone for a smoke, I see him on his phone. Jay returns, yeah, about an hour. I mean for all I know I could be talking to the Police, but I am certain he is not. Jay's phone beeps drink up we're off. The barman gives me a strange look, I am sure he knows what Jay is up to. Who knows, he may even get some commission.

We walk to the car park, a big silver BMW is parked in the corner, with two black guys in the front. We get in the back, the passenger says you got the cash? I hand him £700.00, he counts it and passes me the gear. Jay give him your number in case he needs anymore and we part company. Those two are not to be messed with either.

I find another pub down the road. I am desperate for a line but will wait until I am back in my hotel room. Just killing time now until Graham turns up.

Back in my room, time to try this new gear, bloody hell it is like rocket fuel, I am seeing stars. I am going to stay put here for the next couple of days, it is the lead up to Christmas and that means a lot of pissed up idiots and Police. It is safer to stay put for now, I have started to get the odd nose bleed, it is not worrying me, but no surprise in one way, the amount I have pushed up it. Christmas Day and Boxing Day were very enjoyable, very friendly and welcoming.

The day after Boxing Day it was time to hit the streets again, Graham drops me at the Clock tower around 7.30pm and he will pick me up at 1am. I head straight to the Crown and Anchor, it is very quiet, only 6 or 7 people in. The same guy is behind the bar, Gin and Tonic sir, yes please, he remembers me, then again who could forget me. It is nearly 9 o'clock and I am thinking of moving on when Jay walks in. I buy him a lager and we sit, as we chat I notice two fingers missing on his left hand, what happened? You know the two guys in the BMW, it was them, Why? My Mrs was nagging me for the rent, I didn't have it, so I borrowed it without asking and that is what I get in return. You can do anything with a chisel and a hammer. If I were you I wouldn't hang around here too long, it really isn't a nice place. Just hearing that put my nerves on edge.

I arranged another delivery of coke and then I take him for an Indian. I know he is a thug but underneath he is not a bad guy. He is just trying to make the best of a bad situation. I have seen these posters around Keep Calm and Carry On, well I hope I can carry on. The hotel is lovely, but the rest is not for me, I haven't seen a Rolls or a Bentley since I arrived, my heart belongs in London. However, I am not finished yet, I am a Conman and I am not leaving until I hit gold.

I had a very enjoyable evening with Jay, he and Stuart could add value to me. It is not so much the money or the lording it up over people,

I think it is the thrill of the chase, what a buzz, as I wonder off with anything I fancy. The nose bleeds are concerning me slightly, the coke Jay supplies is pure savage, total madness, I will ease up on it a bit. I open my laptop, just curious to what the horse is worth. I have only found one by the same maker, it's valued at £3,400. Now I have bonded with Stuart, he can sell it for me, I will chuck him £100.00 for his trouble, well worth it and it keeps me out of the frame, if it goes tits up I will deny everything. I have even polished it over to remove my finger prints.

I call room service, roast pork and a bottle of fizz. Stuart arrives 20 minutes later, now's my chance, he pours my Champagne, is there anything else sir? Yes Stuart, what time do you finish tonight? 7pm sir. Can you spare me ten minutes? Yes of course sir, I will see you just after 7pm. I slip him a £10.00 tip, this all helps the buttering up process. Now, he is wondering what do I want with the likes of him.

As I look out over the lake, a small grin sweeps over my face, Lady Penelope would have now realised she has got a worthless cheque for £50,000 in her possession. Then, again I very much doubt if she made her fortune through hard work and honesty, I dread to think how she got it, she has probably behaved worse than me somehow. I know I am a heartless bastard, I don't care who suffers as long as I am ok, that is all that matters.

Stuart taps on my door just at just after 7pm, hello sir how can I help? Please take a seat, he declines a drink, as he is driving. Stuart, I won this horse in a charity auction, it is such a hassle carrying it around everywhere. I have a dealer interested in purchasing it, I wondered if you would take it to him, I will pay you of course. Yes, sir, please call me Adam, it is Hall and Green antiques in West Street. Yes, I know it, I don't live far from there. I am here until 1 o'clock in the afternoon tomorrow. Ok, we agreed on around £2,100. No, problem, leave it with me. Oh, you need to ask for Robin Hall. I will pick it up just after 1 o'clock tomorrow. I will see you then, thank you and he departs. Why have a dog and bark yourself?

Just chilling out, using the swimming pool and jacuzzi, how relaxing, this is where I should be. I have wrapped the horse in a shirt and placed it in a bag careful not to touch it. Stuart is here for the collection, but I will not see him until tomorrow evening when his shift starts. When you are important people want to run around after you, it is great. Let them do the dirty work. Sometimes I honestly do not know why I am like I am, my parents and brother were decent, hardworking people. I think it stems back to watching my father work hard every day and still have nothing to show for it. When we were kids we couldn't even have an ice cream when the van came around. Who said hard work pays, most of these rich and well to do haven't done an honest day's work in their lives, it is all lies and bullshit. If you are poor and middle class you do not count for anything in this country. It is a ladder the rich are getting richer and laughing, the middle class are just there and the poor count for nothing, it has always been the same. I think this is why they play the lottery. However, they have not got the common sense to realise you have no chance of winning. I would rather be dead than poor.

Stuart came to my room as promised handing me an envelope with £2,100 inside. I slipped two fifties into his pocket. Well done, thank you Stuart and he thanked me. You see he is another example of someone working hard every day, almost certainly paid minimum wage and just struggling by. This was a good exercise, I know he can be trusted. Now he has gone, I have a count up, £61,000 in real cash plus my dodgy stuff.

I need more coke, so arrange to meet Jay at the Crown at eight o'clock, another £500 will be sufficient for now. It is well into January and I book the hotel for another two weeks, they give me a 10% discount, for being a good loyal customer, that makes me laugh, me good and loyal. I am building a very good friendship with Stuart, slowly but surely reeling him in. I meet Jay that evening and collect the coke. No problems just how I like it. I am going to offer Stuart a job soon as my PA, it all adds to the mix. People are so busy working 9 to 5 they really do not expect someone like me to creep up behind them.

Back to the hotel. The coke is wild to say the least, I really should ease up on it, but I just cannot man. I take my laptop to the bar, I will have to see if there is any news about me. My password is conman50. This is because I am a conman and I am sure I will be dead by the time I am 50. In my usual position in the corner. It is very quiet, I browse the web, I will try the London Evening Post, generally to see if there is any easy pickings for me. Shit the headline on page two, Conman Fleeces Charity for thousands, a picture of Lady Penelope and two scratchy pictures of me, I know it is me, but the picture quality is very poor. I read on she describes me as "a gentleman, nobody had any reason to doubt him, I would urge him to return the items if he has any decency. Doing this to a charity is absolutely despicable." Also, a picture of the horse and necklace. "Anybody with any information please call crime stoppers on this number" I just pray no one here see's this. Stuart is only a few feet away and I got him to sell the horse. I'm slightly worried now, even if I wanted to return the items I couldn't they were long gone. Oh, I also forgot to mention the Police would like to talk to me regarding numerous frauds in and around the London area. In one way I feel like handing myself in but I know that that is not an option. I will just lie low for a bit, I retreat to my room and smack the coke.

Hopefully, the story will disappear soon. Maybe I was a tad greedy, that night, but what a buzz, they say you either win it, earn it or steal it. Being the selfish greedy little shit, I am I chose to steal it.

I bet all of Doncaster are still doing the same day in day out and still just poor. I am trying to see if there is any way I could see my mother, I am really missing her and Robert. I have looked over social media, but have drawn a blank, having to keep my whereabouts secret doesn't help either. I would just like to know they are alright. Another thing I do know is my money is not going to last forever, especially, the way I spend. For some reason the fun seems to have disappeared, maybe I just need something new, but stay away from charity auctions. The rohypnol hotel scams were good little earners, but there must be something easier, where I do not have to get my hands dirty.

I have decided to get some business cards printed, these will put me in good stead for any future scams. I found a printer in Glasgow, I will get 100 reading Sir Adam Cleaver, Apartment 19 Bignall Mansions, Belgravia, London. With my pay as you go number at the bottom, the cards will help prove who I am. Nice quality white card with gold lettering £143.00, a good investment. I will have them picked up next week.

In town again, I find a nice little wine bar called Bar 90, tucked away down an alley way. it is very pleasant with a nice friendly atmosphere. After 2 Gin and Tonics I head off to the Crown, still have an hour and a half until Graham picks me up. When I enter, Jay is at the bar, I get him a drink and we reside to our normal spot. Jay asks if I need anything, but I am fine now. Jay tells me this area was a no go zone a few years ago, however, it has all changed now, he says there is still plenty of bother here, but nothing like it used to be. Every weekend someone was murdered on this street. Everything has changed now the good old days have gone. Using a sawn-off shot gun to rob a bank, it is all done from your armchair now, the fun has gone out of it.

I ask if Jay knows where I can get my hands on a passport, as I have lost mine and have to travel overseas on business soon. Jay goes outside to make a call, once back inside, no problem, £700.00, two passport photos and your Signature. Give me a week, we arrange to meet in exactly one week. Once we meet it only takes an hour to have the passport made up. Graham collects me at five and I return to the hotel.

I spot Stuart on the hall way, I approach him and ask if he would possibly be able to pick up my printing next Wednesday from Roberts printing in Cornmarket Street. I will pay you for your trouble, Stuart agrees on the spot, I have now proved that I trust him, he has no idea what is coming his way.

I have eased off the coke, I need to think straight. Stuart collects my printing and I meet Jay for my passport. I will only have three days left at the hotel. If my next scam is going to be successful, every detail must slot perfectly into place, one mess up and it is all over.

I am pining to go back to London, but I know it is a nonstarter, for now. There is no way I would even consider Doncaster. I have seen a nice hotel in Devon, The Lord Charles, it is 5 star and £190 a night for a private suite. I will not book it yet, I do not want to tempt fate.

I am really putting some coke away now, I am even rehearsing my next con in my room, like a military exercise I am greedy and want it all, the problem is, what do you do when you have it all, who knows, what a nice problem to have.

My new passport looks perfect, with that and my new cards, I will have people just where I want them. I also need to recoup some of my costs, the cards the passport, have set me back nearly a grand. I am sure the barman in the Crown knows what Jays up to, he would be stupid if he didn't, but he is probably getting a small commission and gets to keep his pub in once piece. I do like Jay, it's as though I have found a friend for once in my miserable life.

When I handed him the money for the passport it was slightly nerve racking, he could have very easily beaten me and run, but he didn't. With my document on board, time to open a bank account, now this will be a big test of nerve. I have got everything I need and I will give them Belgrave as my address. Walking towards the Bank I am a bit shaky and sweaty. A mixture of fear, booze and coke. I feel like turning back but I have to keep going. If for any reason things go wrong I get straight back to the Hotel and scarper, it is always good to have a plan B.

Chapter 7

Once inside the bank I ask for just a standard account to pay in and of course withdraw. I have also grown my beard and got a cap and glasses on. Just a little disguise to help. I pass over £200.00 to open with, after about ten minutes all is done. They give me a temporary sort code, account number and advise if I need to pay in or withdraw I will have to visit a branch until my card arrives in the post. That's all good, we shake hands and I make a quick getaway.

Graham drives me back to the hotel and Stuart is on reception. We say hello and I ask if he would like to join me for a drink later, he accepts and we arrange to meet in my room at 9.30pm, when he finishes. I order room service and two bottles of Champagne. I will just see if the auction story is still there, I can't see it. Perhaps it has fizzled away, the same as all old news.

Another thing I had forgotten about, I still have a very nice Rolex watch in my bag. I am toying with presenting this to Stuart as a gift. I will have to think about that one. Stuart arrives just after 9.30pm, he looks a bit confused as to what I want with him. Well to cut a long story short, I may be leaving soon and when I return to London, how would you feel about working for me? I need a PA and a driver, I will sort out accommodation for you and your family. Also, a nice vehicle and a salary of £50,000. At this point I saw his jaw hit the floor, he is stunned. I don't know what to say. Look talk it over with your wife, I will be looking to appoint somebody in around 7 to 8 weeks' time. Stuart leaves my room jumping for joy, like he has just won the lottery twice.

I even told him he could pick which car he wanted, and I would also cover any nursery costs. It sounds to good to be true, that is because it is. Stuart really thinks he has hit the big time, what a shame he hasn't, he is just another sad victim, as you will find out. But it is nice to give a little encouragement, that is the one thing I never had.

I do ponder for a couple of minutes, how on earth did a nobody from Doncaster get to this? When I was a kid my Mother made me wear my Brothers old shoes, once he had finished with them, even if they had holes in, I wore three pairs of socks, just to keep my feet dry. My clothes were just rags, everything had holes in. My father borrowed money from doorstep lenders, where you borrow £200 and end up paying back £500, with an extortionate interest rate. I feel my parents were in a vicious circle, with no way out.

Now and then a school trip would arise, two weeks skiing in Italy only £900, I didn't even bother taking the letter home, absolutely pointless. Don't get me wrong, we didn't starve, but there certainly wasn't anything spare.

My Grandmother Joyce, that is my father's mother, lived about a mile away. My Grandfather died in 1974, in a car accident, she lived alone in a small bungalow. I would cycle round to see her most weekends, she was a lovely lady, very caring and generous. If she had it she would give it to you. I never once took advantage of her, I knew she had next to nothing, she gave me time and that meant more to me than anything. I think she believed it was fine to have nothing and remain on the bottom, definitely not for me though.

I clearly remember one episode, I was only either 8 or 9, I went to town shopping with her, as we left the Chemist, a young man was lying on the floor with a dirty blanket over him, next to a rubbish bin, he was very dirty. People were giving him a wide birth, not my Grandmother, she walked over to him, I am holding her hand trying to pull her back, I did feel a bit frightened, I don't want to be anywhere near him. My Gran stoops down, are you alright love? He mumbled something back, I didn't hear what it was as I was six or seven feet away. She returned to me holding my hand, poor love, I thought we were going home, we went into a bakery across the square and she bought a tea and a pasty, she opens her purse and pays. I saw that her purse was now virtually empty, all that is left is our bus tickets home. We return to the guy and Gran hands him the tea and pasty; the guy is so grateful, and we left to get the bus. That was my granny, she would give you anything, even when she didn't have it. Sadly, she passed away in

1992. I am 25 now and still miss her so much. Rest in peace Gran, god bless you. What a kind lovely lady, I have come to the conclusion that if I ever had a family, not much chance of that, my children would certainly not have holes in their shoes. Maybe it was a sign of the times, looking back I feel quite deflated and depressed, I know she would very much disagree with my life style, but I can hear her say, for goodness sake be careful love.

One thing though is apart from Pete's mum, years ago, I haven't ripped off anyone who couldn't afford it. I would love to see Gran again, but on the other hand I am glad she doesn't know what I am up to.

It is cold wet and grey out there, this also makes me feel a bit down. I have a line and that sorts me out nicely. I am still getting the odd nose bleed and getting headaches, I blame the booze and coke.

I just had a count up, £51,000 left. Christ, I have spent some since being here, no wonder they gave me 10% discount off. Also, in the bottom of my bag, I see my cheque book and rohypnol, these will come in handy at some point. By now I am usually looking at different types of scam, but I just cannot seem to concentrate, my mind keeps drifting. One day I am sure this will all come to an end. What would I do? Where would I end up? But things are going well, so don't worry about it for now. If I did get caught, there is no justice in this country, I would probably only get two or three years and what a better place to make new contacts than prison.

What would stop me from doing it all over again, I only started with £600. Opportunities just keep on coming, I have just seen a lovely Ferrari pull up outside, private number plates. It must be well over a hundred grand sat there. I see Graham looking at it so I join him outside. Who's is this Graham? It belongs to Mr Shaw, he owns a haulage company in Leeds. He stays here on business. I get Graham to take a photo on my phone, with me standing next to it. The picture is excellent, I am very pleased.

Back in my room I contact the website people and request this new picture be added. They said it may take 24 hours, that's fine. See what I mean about opportunities, I was straight on it, no time to waste. It's only a side view picture, I don't want anyone to see the number plate. Yes, it is the small things that lead to the big things. Anyhow, I am looking at loans, there is literally hundreds on here, if I can pull this one off I want a minimum of £60,000. Just doing little research for now, cannot see any problems, I have everything I need, apart from someone else's personal details, that shouldn't be much of a problem though.

Chapter 8

It is now Wednesday, I am only paid up until Friday, so on Saturday my next destination will be Devon. I meet Jay again for more coke that afternoon, I tell him I may be leaving soon but I will stay in touch and look him up if I return, not much chance of that. I thank him for all he has done, and we part company.

I arrive back around 6pm, hide the coke in my room and head off downstairs to the restaurant. I have a perfectly cooked steak and a bottle of wine. Stuart arrives to take my plate away. Sorry to bother you Sir, would I possibly be able to have a quick word with you later? Yes of course when ever you are free, about 20 minutes later he returns.

Stuart and his wife, Laura, are inviting me to their house for a meal tomorrow evening at 7pm, yes that would be lovely, thank you. Oh, Graham knows where I live. I will bring a bottle. Thank you, see you at 7. Now I have got him just where I want him, things are falling nicely into place, all systems go. This could be my best payday yet. This is how my evening with Stuart and Laura goes.

I must have taken over an hour to get ready, very light makeup. Admiring myself in the full-length mirror, highly polished Oxford brogues, designer jeans, white shirt, navy blue suit jacket, with of course a silk handkerchief in my top pocket, yes perfection. You could just see me stepping into a sparkling Rolls Royce, I look stunning if I say so myself. What an arrogant little bastard, I am. Reception call and my car is ready when I am. I will make him wait, a few minutes, that's what usually happens when you are an important person. A good splash of Armani and off we go.

On the way I tell Graham to stop at the shop, I purchase two bottles of Champagne and some flowers for his wife, a nice gesture I think. I did lay into the girl on the till, £82.80, excuse me do you have no manners. Oh, very sorry, that is £82.80, please sir. Yes, that is better, you should learn some respect. I paid in cash and left. I may be a con artist, liar and cheat, but I am certainly never rude to anybody.

Now approaching Stuarts house, we are in a large housing estate, it looks quite new and very tidy. As soon as I'm near the front door Stuart opens it. I apologise for being a little late, no problem sir, please come in. Please call me Adam. This is my wife Laura. Hello, pleased to meet you, I greet her with a light kiss on each cheek. I hand over the Champagne and roses, you didn't have to, no it is my pleasure, thank you for inviting me. I would guess Laura is around 30, brown shoulder length hair and glasses, a very pretty girl by all accounts.

We sit in a small but cosy dining room, I see a baby monitor on and pictures on the walls. I didn't know you had children Laura. Yes, just the one, Annabel, she will be 2 in a couple weeks. Oh, how lovely. Then Stuart appears with 3 glasses of Champagne, dinner will be served in half and hour, is that ok, yes of course. We sit and make small talk. You see I am used to Champagne, they are not. When it starts hitting them, I will gather the information I need, and they will not suspect a thing.

We have a lovely dinner and move into the sitting room. So, how long have you worked at the Hotel? Just 4 years now. I always found that if I ask someone a question and receive an answer, if I keep looking at them they always tell you more. Before that I was at Clarke and Son's Menswear, in the town, but they closed. Mr Clarke retired, and his son didn't want to carry on, I really enjoyed. But the Hotels good and very easy going.

I have spotted a letter behind a picture on the fireplace. I will have a look when I get the chance. Graham is collecting me at 11.30, is that ok? Yes of course. What a lovely house you have, how long have you lived here? We moved in May 2012. I was always trying to guess how old you are Stuart. How old do you think I am? 28-29. Nearly, I am 34. Laura and I are both 34, my birthday is on the 4th January and hers is the 9th July. I don't want to seem like I am questioning them, they just keep throwing information my way and very grateful I am too. Laura works eighteen hours a week as a dental nurse. Oh, which one? Jefferies and Schofield in the high street, it's been there over twenty years. I have only been with them for 7 months, Annabel is a full-time job on her own.

Second bottle now open, they tell me everything and more, I am not even trying it's now 9.40pm. I ask about my job offer, they say they are very interested and still thinking about it. All the same, even if they refuse my offer I have invited them to stay at my Oxfordshire mansion in the summer as my work load eases, they jump at the chance. I may be leaving soon but if you give me your contact details, I can get in touch. Laura writes down their email address, both mobile numbers and the house landline. This couldn't be easier, no effort needed whatsoever. I can hear Annabel stirring over the monitor, Laura goes upstairs to see to her and Stuart is off to the toilet, leaving me to roam free for a minute. I can hear they are both with Annabel. I grab the letter from behind the picture, get my phone and take a snap of it, return it and sit back where I was, not sure what it was. It looked like a letter from the Bank. I will have a look next time I go to the toilet.

Is she alright? As if I care, yes just a little restless, she is back to sleep now. Can I use your toilet please? Yes of course, straight up the stairs and on your right. Once inside, door locked tight, phone out, it is a Council Tax bill, this will do nicely. Snort half a line and return downstairs.

I try not to reveal too much about myself. When you are a conman the less you tell the better, you have to have an excellent memory. Just to keep on top of things, they are a truly lovely family, something else I missed out on. They honestly don't deserve the carnage and misery I am going to inflict on them. I even know where he and Laura were born and even what their parents do for a living.

It's 11.30pm and Graham is waiting for me. I thank them for such a lovely evening. We will be in touch about your offer and I depart back to the Hotel. I am just like a magpie swoop in take what I want and gone.

In my room laptop out, right let's have a look at some loans, it's gone midnight. Anything between forty and sixty grand would do. I have applied for nine totalling just over £65,000. I gave all Stuarts details, but use my mobile number and account details. Within half an hour, I get confirmation that I have been accepted for £28,000 and funds will be in my account within hours. No choice but to wait on the others, I may get a phone call regarding this.

I start to pack up, I need a quick get away in the morning. I won't use Graham, so I book another firm to be here at 9am. It is now after 2am and I am feeling very tired. All packed up now, I set my alarm for 7am. Being a fraudster can really take its toll on you. I know the coast will be clear in the morning. Stuart doesn't start work until 1 o'clock, I will be long gone by then. One last check on the loan situation and I have been accepted on four more, I am now up to £43,000, great that's where I wanted to be, anything else is a bonus.

Up at 7am, shower, dress and down breakfast, it is just after 8am, only an hour to go. I had a quick look, there is no more activity on the loans. But I am happy with what I have got. Five to nine and I am in reception with my 3 holdalls making pleasantries with the staff. I say I will stay again next time I am up here, you must be joking. My phone rings, it's the Taxi company apologising my driver is running 15 minutes late, nothing I can do, just wait. I am starting to panic a bit and feel sweaty. I hope this all works out, not a good start. I have yet to go to the bank, just keep your cool and stay calm. Finally, my taxi arrives, bags in the boot and gone.

Next stop Nat West in the town. I get the driver to wait around the corner, it is just after 10 o'clock, this is a big one, if I am rumbled, it could be the end of the game. Once inside the bank there is four people in the que. My hands are shaking, and I feel sweat running down my back. The paranoia is also taking hold, I am sure everybody is looking at me. I look at it as a game of poker, luckily for me I have won every time, but if I lose I am not just going home quids down and slightly pissed off, I will end up inside. Finally, now at the cashier's window, I ask for a balance, she asks for my card, then I explain that I am still waiting for it but I have got my account number and sort code, also my passport. Yes, that is fine, after a couple of seconds she passes me a slip of paper, £43,407, ok, may I withdraw £43,000 please. Yes of course, I will just check with the manager. On her return she shows me into a side room, just for privacy, that's fine sir, how would you like your money? I ask for half in twenty's and half in fifty's, just a bit less to carry around. She offers me tea or coffee, which I politely decline. I may be 5 or 10 minutes, that was the longest wait of my life. I am sweating like a pig, I'm a right mess. Finally, she returns with two large envelopes, all I need is your signature, I scribble as quick as possible and walk very calmly out, thanking them as I leave.

The cold air hits me and I shiver, I'm dripping in cold sweat, I wipe my face with a handkerchief and return to the taxi, to the station please. I sit slumped down behind the passenger seat, envelopes stuffed inside my coat. On arrival I stuff the cash in the bottom of my holdall, pay the fare with a generous tip and walk into the station. I'm beaming with delight, give myself a pat on the back, how easy was that. I have decided to put Devon on hold for now. I'm longing to see my mother, she always had my best interests at heart all those years ago, it wasn't all her fault. I really would like to tell her that she is a good woman who certainly deserved better. I don't even know if she received my letter when I was in Surrey.

Now in the station all the trains are delayed except one to Birmingham, this will have to do, it leaves in forty minutes. I know I cannot hang around here, so ticket booked and find a corner to hide. It's very cold and damp, I'm not feeling well either. Now finally on my way, there is a couple of people on here, that suits me fine. I desperately need a line, the only place is the toilet, but I cannot leave my bag unattended, I will just have to take it with me. I just hope when I am in Birmingham there is a train to Doncaster. All of a sudden, my plans seem to be up in the air, but I am sure I will be alright.

Chapter 9

I have arrived in Birmingham, there is a train, but it is in an hour. I spot a pub on the corner and sit and wait. It's a grubby old dump but I am only wasting time. If I get to see my mother and she knows about my wrong doings, all I can do is deny everything and say I have been working overseas. I take this chance to listen to my voicemails. There are some very disgruntled people wanting to talk to me, Stuart being one and loan companies as well. One loan company is saying your money will be in your account by the end of the day, how lovely, thank you. I will find another bank tomorrow. One thing I must do is get a new sim card for my phone and dump this one.

It has been seven years since I saw my mother, I just hope she got rid of that loser Gary. I also wonder how Robert is, last I knew him and his girlfriend had a flat somewhere in Liverpool. Feeling exhausted, it's been a very long day, but also very profitable, so it's worth it. I have left the pub and only ten minutes to wait and I will be on my way home.

I am finally at Doncaster station, it's 7.40pm, very cold and dark. God this miserable place hasn't changed. Only a short cab ride to my old house. I take a card from the driver, I will probably need him later. Now at the old house, how bleak, the gate is hanging off, the grass is knee high and in total darkness. First impression, I think it is empty. I do ring the bell six or seven times, but nothing.

Just as I am going to walk away old Mr Blake appears from next door. They have lived there for longer than I can remember. Hello, Adam is that you? Hello, Mr Blake, I have come to see my mother, but it doesn't appear to be anyone in. He invites me in, Mrs Blake is in the kitchen, and kindly makes me a cup of tea. We sit in the kitchen and Mrs Blake reveals that Gary ran off with a woman from the corner shop over two years ago. My mother sold the house to a builder, packed up and left about a year ago, she didn't tell us where she is going. We have no contact details for her whatsoever.

I feel very upset seeing the house empty and not knowing her whereabouts. Would things have been different if I had stayed, something I will never know. I then ask if they knew anything about Robert. All they knew is he was living somewhere in Liverpool. They do know he and his girlfriend had a baby a few years back but that's it. I explain I have been working overseas for long periods of time and just lost contact.

Time is cracking on, there is no point in being here, so I phone the cabby to come back for me. I thank Mr and Mrs Blake and depart. Back in the cab, I know a small village called Greythorne, it is about 20 miles from here. I book into the Kings

Arms Hotel, it is an old coaching Inn, a bit basic but cosy. I just need to rest and sort out my next move.

Sitting in the bar it is the lowest I have felt for quite some time. Having a look at my laptop I cannot see anything about me, but there is time yet. I feel myself sinking into a real miserable depression, all I think I truly want is that one person to love me and be normal. A job, house and all the other odds and ends that go with it. I am really not in a good place at the moment and I do conclude, yes in fact I do blame my parents. In fact, I would have had at least a fighting chance if I had of been adopted. People may think I am just looking for someone to blame, but I think I am right. I cannot even think of anything good about my childhood, memories, holidays, school, nothing. Robert and myself didn't get on, to be honest we were two totally different people. It makes me wonder if we even had the same father. That is something else that has always been in the back of my mind and I doubt if I will ever know. But whatever happens, all the same, I do wish him well and every success. I even have a nephew somewhere out there. Hopefully, one day we can all meet again, deep down the chances of that are very slim.

The only person who may have any insight on the whereabouts of my mother and Robert is Aunt Ruby, she really is the last person I want to talk to. We didn't part on the best of terms and why would she want to help me in anyway, shape or form. Perhaps this is a lesson in how not to burn your bridges. But, if I want to find anything out I have no choice.

Still trying to think of my next destination, I cannot stay here, there is literally nothing, just a tiny village with a cricket green and post office. Devon would be desolate this time of year, plus I would stick out like a sore thumb. I am really only left with one choice and that is return to London. It is very risky, but it is the one layout I know well. This time I will have to stay away from the centre and keep more, let's say, less reckless approach.

That night I really smash the coke and booze. I just cannot stop, it is 2am and still going strong, I'm absolutely battered. I cannot see straight, let alone stand up. I will contact Aunt Ruby, but not when I am like this.

Chapter 10

I finally decide on Oxford, there is a very nice hotel and I would blend in nicely with the college boys. It is always busy, that is a good thing. I am going to travel by car, money is no object, I have got, let's say, more than I need. The receptionist books me a car, I think she is a bit shocked, Oxford, yes that is what I said, ok sir. Well it is a very long way from here, she was just shocked I suppose. When I arrive, I will get the rest of my money from the bank and find another sim for my phone, then just try and relax for a couple of days.

It is a bright but cold afternoon and in Oxford I got rid of the rest of my toy town money on the taxi driver, he dropped me off a couple of miles from the Centre, then I jumped on a bus and now in the Hotel. It is very posh, five star, not cheap but lavish, that is just what I need right now. I am only booking for two nights, I know I cannot be in the same place too long.

First stop the bank, my balance is £10,733, I withdraw £10,000 and disappear. I think now I have around £90,000 in cash, now sim cards, that is easy done. I do need more coke, so I find a nice little pub down an alley way, in a corner, it is very quiet in here, if I say so myself, I feel awful after last night, hopefully a couple of drinks will square me up. I swop sims, only keeping my Aunt Ruby's number, I discard the others. I will bin the old card when I leave. Two guys are at the bar, obviously students, they are younger than me, a bit scruffy looking. There are loads of spare tables, but they choose to sit right next to me. As I said before, I don't have to look for anyone, they come to me.

After about 15 minutes or so they introduce themselves as Spencer and Rupert. They are both studying Law, this really did tickle me, how bazar. Hello, I am Adam, I will drop the Sir for now. They seem like a couple of idiots to me, the sort that have wealthy parents and just don't want to work, so they have ended up here. I generally tell them nothing. Spencer retreats outside for a cigarette and I buy them both a drink, I take a chance to ask Rupert if he knows anywhere I can obtain some coke, he joins Spencer outside and on return says, can you meet me outside Pizza House at 7.30pm tonight? Yes, of course. How much do you want? £200.00 worth? No problem, they drink up, see you tonight. These two are very easy prey, no effort needed at all, they really are as stupid as they look. I know he will only give me £150.00 worth and pocket the other £50, or so he thinks. Someone is going to suffer, but it certainly won't be me.

We meet as arranged at 7.30pm, he is on his own, follow me, it is at my flat, it is too risky out here, there are cameras everywhere. We walk about 20 minutes to a block of flats, we enter, even the hallway stinks of piss, god knows what his flat will be like. Once inside it is shocking, the smell, the dirt, the mess, it is utterly disgusting, he hands me a tin of larger and I pass him £200.00. When he leaves to fetch the gear, I drop rohypnol into his can, he passes me the gear and I strike up a low-key conversation, within half an hour he is really wobbly and finally hits the floor. I do a quick look around to see if there is anything worth taking, but definitely not, he is out cold. I retrieve my cash from his pocket and bid him farewell. Most dealers use guns and violence, I am more advanced, let's say, not so reckless.

My god I need a shower and change, that was the pits. I have never encountered a place like that before, you certainly know students live there. He fell for that big style, what an idiot. You would never catch me living like that, not in a million years, I would rather be dead.

I had, maybe, a close shave earlier going back to my hotel, walking up the high street, out of nowhere, two Policemen are walking towards me, I really didn't see them until it was too late. I had my cap and glasses on and quickly grabbed my handkerchief from my top pocket and pretended to start sneezing. They didn't even look at me and kept walking. But they are only beat bobbies, they have probably never heard of me, I am sure they will one day.

Lying on my four-poster bed, waiting for room service to arrive, I am feeling more than pleased with myself, also quite ill, very sweaty and still the nose bleeds are getting more and more frequent. I know that deep down I am only going to end up in one of three places, prison, dead or in rehab, if I could choose it would be rehab, but the way I carry on it is a pure throw of the dice. I am still not a 100% sure as to whether to contact Aunt Ruby, this really is tormenting me now, shall I or shan't I. The coke plays tricks with me, telling me, go on, then best not to. I have promised myself that I am definitely going to make a decision in the morning.

Oxford is a different world from the Scotland Hotel, it is more like a miniature London, out of the two I think I prefer Scotland. By the way, this coke I acquired from Spencer isn't the best, but it was free, so thanks all the same. Tomorrow is another day and I do admit it is nice to do as I please and having the money to do it. Being stuck in a factory or office all day just doesn't appeal to me whatsoever, even at school, which I hated immensely, I felt like a caged animal, at least I am free now.

One place I forgot to mention where I probably will end up, is hell. Browsing the web, Glasgow news, fraudster cons hotel worker out of thousands, accompanied by two pictures of me, obviously from the Hotel CCTV cameras. They don't name Stuart, but they do me. They have connected me with the auction scam, as well as many others. I am, definitely, now wanted. My time here is coming to an end, I must look for my next destination. I cannot help but wonder what would have been if Gwen were still here. Then again, I have a habit of pissing people off after a while, so it probably wouldn't have lasted.

I have also noticed that my web page has been removed, I am very angry about that, so I telephone them to be told the reason for removal was fraudulent activity on the account. I strongly deny this and demand it be reinstated but to no avail. I think it is time to move on tomorrow. I know of a place called Stokenchurch, between here and London. On the web there is a nice-looking hotel there, that is my next stop.

Up at eight. Shower, breakfast, in my room packing doesn't take long, I haven't really got much. Sad in one way, I am out by 9am and grab the first cab, on my way I do realise I won't be able to run forever, I feel like the net is closing in.

I have used this hotel before, it is nicely tucked away, and I am familiar with the layout, plus it is only half an hour from London. I used it as a hideout a couple of years ago, when things were getting a bit heavy in town. I have decided to call Aunt Ruby this afternoon, I really don't fancy it, but I have no choice.

I am at the Eagle Hotel in just under an hour, it still looks the same. It is really just a pit stop, check in for two nights and go up to my room, it is not as plush as some I have frequented, but it is fine for now. It is freezing outside, dark and grey, very depressing. But I am absolutely roasting, it is as if I am on fire, I am sure there is something wrong, now and then I look slightly yellow. But I have no chance in seeing a doctor, the last doctor I saw was in Doncaster when I was 12 years old, I slipped on the ice and cracked a bone in my elbow. If I ease up a bit perhaps things may get better.

To some people my lifestyle may seem very appealing, unlimited money, fine food in exclusive restaurants, chauffer driven cars, top hotels, but it is not all as glamorous as it seems. When I turn the light off at night, I am on my own, a wanted man looking over my shoulder 24 hours a day. It is a very lonely existence, I certainly wouldn't recommend it.

Chapter 11

After lunch I finally find the courage to call my Aunt Ruby, my hands are shaking, well trembling, I am not sure what kind of reception awaits me. Well it's ringing, don't turn back now, she answers, hello Aunty it's Adam, oh how are you, yes fine thank you and yourself, yes, I am ok, how can I help? I have just come back from working overseas and I dropped by to see mother, only to find that she has now moved. I spoke with the neighbours and nobody seems to know her whereabouts. I just wondered if you knew where she may be? Yes, I do, that Gary ran off and left her, she sold the house and bought a flat in a village called Wrenslaid, not far from Brighton, do you have a pen? I'll give you her number, I'll just fetch it. I write it down, thank you so much, you really must pop in next time you're in town, yes of course and the conversation ended.

I was expecting a real grilling, that just didn't seem right at all, I caused and gave her a lot of grief, it just doesn't add up. Well, at least I did it and finally have mothers number, I try a couple of times and it goes straight to voicemail, I don't leave a message. I will try again in a bit.

Nearly just had a heart attack, I have just seen a Police car outside, panic over, they are stopping speeders, that just shows how close things are, I am maybe 100 feet away, if only they knew, but it is well known that they are more interested in catching someone for no tax or Insurance, than hunting down murderers or rapists, anything for an easy ride and pull in some money at the same time. I bet if I walked past them they wouldn't even look at me, I really don't have any time whatsoever for them. I remember years ago, I may have only been 9 or 10, my father was stopped one evening on his way home from work, he had a back light out, which he knew absolutely nothing about, and they threw the book at him, no warning or advice, just a fine and some points. Disgusting the way, they treated my dad.

There was a pub on the edge of Doncaster, called the Bell, and it was a very well-known fact that Policemen were in there until all hours, fucking hypocrites. This is now when I give them the slip it cheers me up no end, useless assholes, they couldn't find their way out of a paper bag. Anyway, enough about them, I will have some lunch and when they are gone, get some painkillers from the Chemist down the road.

I so hope I can meet with my mother, it has been a lot of years now, also I would like to find out where Robert is and what he is up to, it would be lovely to see him again and my nephew that I have never met. Just had lunch and 4 pain killers, washed down by three gin and tonics. Back in my room I sleep for a couple of hours, well more like a pass out, it is now late afternoon, I look in the bathroom mirror, I look awful, bloodshot eyes, tired generally haggard, I will wait for another hour and try her again.

For some reason, I get really worked up and agitated by the most stupid things, seeing those cops or my room service is running 5 minutes late, sitting in traffic, I cannot explain it, little things annoy me so much. I have finally spoken with my mother for the first time in 17 years. I left home when I was eighteen and I am 35 now, so yes it must be. She actually thought I was dead, where has the time gone? I did ask how Robert was and she said we will have a good chat when we meet, we arranged to meet in a pub called The Grapes on Annaswell Lane, in her village, between 2.30pm and 3 o'clock tomorrow. I am absolutely ecstatic, I cannot wait, will I even notice her? Will she notice me?

I telephone down to reception, to inform them that I will be checking out tomorrow and I don't need a refund, as I was paid up for another night and if they could arrange a car to take me to Wrenslaid at 11 o'clock tomorrow morning. Now I must use the time to clean myself up a bit, best foot first, not arrive pissed and high. It will take some doing but I will try my best. You see one major issue I have had over the years it's been just me, there has been no one to reign me in or tell me to stop, that has probably been half my problem, if I need more coke or money I would think nothing of prostituting myself around hotels until I had enough. Awful really, or just cheat someone it is all I knew. I am so happy now, it makes me realise how bloody miserable I have been.

The next morning, I am ready for the off, I knew I would be getting 101 questions fired at me, so I will have to be prepared. Also remember what I have said, so I will have to stay on top of my game. I have just checked out and a guy called John is waiting for me, holdalls in the boot and off I go.

I arrive in Wrenslaid by 2 o'clock. What a quaint little place, very pretty, old thatched cottages, village green, post office, totally unspoilt. By the looks of things, yes this would definitely suit me, I could be lord of the manor, anyhow, now at the Grapes. A very old pub, maybe 17th Century, old oak beams, open fire roaring away. I am a bit early, so gin and tonic and my 3 holdalls and into a corner I go. There is only a handful of people in here, but straight away I can smell money, this is a very well to do place. There are no rollers or Ferrari's outside. It is what I call tucked away cash.

I have been in here for about 20 minutes, I am so nervous, as if I am going to have all of my teeth removed at the dentist. My hands are shaking, to the point, I will only sip my drink when no one is looking. The barman looks me up and down a few times, probably because I am a stranger in these parts. I am at the bar ordering another drink and the door opens, a woman enters, short dark hair, wearing a trouser suit. I glance over and look away, I have to keep an eye on my bags, one is stuffed full of cash. The woman approaches, Adam? Mother? We embrace with tears in our eyes, I get her a glass of wine and return to the corner. We are both amazed at how we have both changed, I was a scrawny, scruffy, pale specimen, now filled out, very smart and tidy. Mother was plump, long hair which always looked greasy and untidy, wow now look at her. The first question from her was where have you been? Well I'd had my fill of Doncaster and as you know Aunt Ruby offered me to stay. Then I lived with a woman for a short time, sadly she passed away. After that I got a job offer from a bank in Hong Kong and that is where I have been most of the time. I am single, I am too busy to have a relationship. Mostly bullshit but what else could I say. Well my main occupation is stealing and defrauding anyone I can.

So, what made you move down here? Well Gary started drinking heavy and would roll in at all hours. Now and then I would get a back hander off him, depending on his mood. This went on for 6 or 7 months, then one Friday morning, he told me he didn't love me anymore and was moving out. By Sunday evening he was gone, the last I heard of him he had lost his job for turning up drunk and was living with another woman, still somewhere around town. I reveal, he was the main reason for me leaving, I couldn't stand him. The reason I didn't say anything, I knew it would have just fallen on deaf ears, which I am certain it would have been the case.

I have lived here for just over two years, there was nothing left for me there. I managed to buy the house from the council and a local builder made me a good offer, so I took it. I did go back a short while ago and Mr Blake filled me in as much as he could. I just had to have a fresh start and it is almost definitely the best thing I have ever done. I have managed to buy my flat outright and still have enough to put a side for my pension.

I found a job straight away, Assistant Manager of Conway's Garden Centre, it is only 20 minutes' walk and I really enjoy it. In one way I am rather pissed off listening to her, how well she is doing and landed on her feet. Quite resentful in one way, if she only knew the truth. I am an alcoholic, cocaine addict, who to cut a long story short, has had an absolute shit life since day one. She is my mother, it was her job to look after me, which I think she failed totally. This is an issue I am sure will always haunt me, even a sorry would be nice.

How is Robert, is he still in Liverpool with Claire? Her face dropped and there was a sudden pause, you don't know do you, I had no way of getting hold of you. Robert died 3 years ago, in a wood yard, close to where they lived, he was working night shifts as a supervisor. I remember it like it was yesterday. It was a Thursday night, about 3am and he said he didn't feel well, a bad headache and felt sick, so he went home. This was very out of character, he never had a day off or was sick. When Claire got up on Friday morning, she found him lying on the sofa, with a blanket over him. She just thought he was asleep, she kept trying to wake him. Eventually, she called an ambulance, once they arrived, straight away they confirmed he was dead. They did a post mortem and confirmed he had suffered a massive stroke. I am so sorry love, I was dreading telling you. I had no way of getting hold of you. I have got tears rolling down my cheeks, I cannot believe it, for once I am totally lost for words. He had a very small funeral, it was a nice sunny day, with just close family and friends. He is buried next to your Grandparents.

What happened to Claire? We lost touch, I have left messages and written, but nothing. That is all I know, I am not even sure if she is still in Liverpool. I tried for a long time, then eventually gave up. I have changed my phone number so many times, for obvious reasons, there was no way she could get hold of me, this is one thing I cannot blame her for. So, it is just the two of us now, oh and Barney. Who's Barney? Please don't tell me she is with someone, he is my little jack Russell, he is six years old. The people in the flat below were moving abroad, so I said I would take him, he is really good company. It can get lonely, being on your own. Tell me about it, I know only too well about being lonely.

She wants to know more about me, but I don't want to tell her, I swerve most of her questions. I ask if she has spoken to Aunt Ruby lately?

Hoping she says no, not for a long time now. I am glad to hear it. You must have done well, just look at your clothes. Yes, I made good investments, at the right time and it paid off. I tell her I have not long sold a villa I had in Portugal, but don't have another place yet. I just use hotels, as I am always on the move with work. She insists on me staying with her, I'm not sure if it is a good idea, but she won't take no for an answer. If it gets too much I will just disappear, just see how it goes. Who knows she may even ask me to invest some cash for her.

I am truly devasted to hear that Robert has gone, I feel guilty now I should have made an effort to meet up with him. But I am a self-centred, selfish person, who doesn't give anyone else much thought. I do think my mother owes me. We leave the pub and go to her flat. Barney is a bit yappy but I'm sure we will get on ok. It is very nice, not very old, clean and tidy. Tenfold better than the squalor of the Doncaster house, in fact, this would do me.

There is someone at the door, this worries me, second floor flat, nowhere to run. It's ok. Who is it? Only George from next door, he lets Barney out when I am at work and I buy him tobacco. He is on his own, no family, no visitors that I have ever seen. I feel quite sorry for him. Yeah, what about me?

My room is small, but tidy and basic, it is fine. That evening we go to a Chinese restaurant in a neighbouring village and just talk. I tell her I have eight weeks off, it is all very nice here, an excellent hiding place, but what the hell am I going to do here. There is only one pub and that is about it. On the other hand, London is not that far away, I am sure I can keep myself entertained somehow.

We return shortly before 11 o'clock, she has work in the morning, so this will give me a chance to have a snoop around. She is now in bed. I want another drink, after a quick search, I come across a bottle of Brandy. Half a tumbler full and a very quick line, I am sorted for bed. I will just have a quick look at my laptop. Still wanted, plus a couple more stories, now the antiques dealers appeared, who Stuart sold the horse to. It may be sensible to keep a low profile here. It is a small place. I could easily be recognised. It is maybe more risk being here than London.

The next morning, and off she goes, a great chance to have a nose about. I cannot help feeling that I am entitled to some compensation, after all it is me that has suffered all these years. I start by sifting through the draws in the living room, nothing. I know there is nothing in my room, I have already checked that last night. The only place left is here, maybe a thousand to one. I also see a couple of old photos, one of me and Robert, when we were at primary school, stood next to dad's car. Also, my Grandparents at an Anniversary party and my mum and dad stood in our old back garden. I have never seen any of these before. I feel quite sad that the only people I cared about and most of them are gone now. I place them back as they were and continue my search.

Wardrobe next, just clothes and some boxes. As I open the first it has got my old scout uniform in, a shudder rips through me, I am sure it was binned, A couple of photo albums, I might have a look at some point. A chest of draws, just clothes. Then bedside table, some paperwork and bank statements, it looks as though she gets by very comfortably. Now a Building Society Savings Book, she has just over £17,000 tucked away. It looks like it was paid in and nothing has ever been withdrawn, now I am starting to reveal the true situation.

Seeing the scout uniform has really upset me. The memories and nightmares are racing back. It was horrific, the way I was abused. Maybe, I should have told someone, I was only a kid, no one would have believed me, over them, and was it for the best that my parents never knew. It would have destroyed everybody's life, not just mine.

We spend the next few days talking, and she gets some old photo albums out. This I think, sends me into a small depression, don't get me wrong, it wasn't all bad, just the majority. I have been here only a couple of days, I'm in need to be out, I'll go bloody mad being cooped up in here. She has given me a key, so I can come and go as I please. A quiet few days is fine, but I need excitement, a challenge, a chase. I decide I am going to float into London on Friday and return on Saturday, a business meeting in the City, well that is what I have told her anyway. A company car will be collecting me at 1 o'clock, but not sure on my return.

Chapter 12

1 o'clock arrives, and I am off, I am quite excited, it seems like ages since I have been in town. I still have to be on my guard though, I have £3,000 on me, more than enough for a good night out. I hide the rest in the loft, safely tucked away Not too long and I get Charles the driver to drop me off at the Majestic in Kensington. I take his number, he can take me back tomorrow.

The bar is nearly empty, I will give it a couple of hours and decide to move on. I need some action, a buzz and is wasn't going to happen here. I feel half cut, just thinking, my next stop will be the Hairy Pair in Soho, Gwen and I went there years ago. A short ride across town, it is now early evening, the place is half full, you have every walk of life in here, gay, straight couples, transgender, that is what I like about it, you can just be yourself with no hassle. I do remove my tie though.

Into a corner booth, £100 bottle of champagne in an ice bucket and lets just see what happens. My eyes scan the clientele, no one sticks out really, perhaps they think the same about me. Perhaps I am being a little impatient, I am used to getting my own way. The place is filling up and I have just clocked a guy looking over. I am not looking at him, but I know he is showing me some interest, this game goes on for about 15 minutes, he is tall and slim, short dark hair and well dressed. Perhaps Greek, I'm not sure. I decide to make a move, I don't want to lose this one.

I wave him over; would you like to join me? He takes a seat next to me, yes he's hot, everything about him. He introduces himself as Roddy, short for Roderick and I am Adam, pleased to meet you. Would you like a glass of Champagne? Yes, thank you. I have a feeling this will be a very good night. I could be sat at my mothers flat with a cup of coco. I don't know if it is fair that I inflict myself on him, but I will try not to. Is this who I have been looking for, the one person, seems ironic he is here, this was one of my first haunts.

My mind is working overtime, I have only known him 10 minutes. If I could whisk him away and settle down I think I would grab it with both hands and certainly not let, go. We have the usual small talk, he reveals he is a physiotherapist at the private Queen Ann Hospital and lives with his father in Chelsea. Straight away I smell money and he is 33 years old. Time now for my bullshit, I am a Director of a Construction Company and only in town tonight. I had a meeting earlier but have another in Brighton tomorrow, really going back to my mothers. I don't want to fuck this one up, ending up full of booze and doing or saying something stupid. I haven't eaten since lunch and this place is packed, so we decide to go for an Italian, I know a nice one only a couple of streets from here.

Roddy, says it is strange he hasn't seen any Police tonight, usually they walk round with dogs, sniffing out drugs. At that point I stalled, shit, I have got coke on me, that would have been the end of the game, how careless, it never crossed my mind. I ask Roddy, if he uses anything, just a little hash at weekends, I can't afford anything else. To that I reply, it is ok I have got plenty and his face lit up.

We have a table for two in the corner, my usual position and I really sense a very strong connection between us. If you are straight and read this you may not understand, but to a gay man he is gorgeous. Definitely, Miss World of gay men. Being so complicated, as I am, I am not over sure how or where he would fit in, perhaps I would have to change? It's getting late and with the excitement of finding him I have forgotten to book a hotel room. Roddy insists I stay with him, I refuse time after time. His father is away, and he has a massive house to himself, he is nearly begging me. I do want to stay, of course, maybe just playing hard to get. I didn't want to show that I am easy prey. The night had only just begun.

I pay the bill and jump into a black cab, to Richmond Street Chelsea, I am like a greyhound waiting to come out of the trap. As we are pulling up, you can smell and taste the wealth here, massive four/five storey houses, Rolls Royce, Bentleys, it is all here and more. Christ talk about a kid in a sweet shop. We enter, the first thing you see are oil paintings, silver, the quality, the grand piano. I am lost for words, now that is not like me. This place has 14 rooms including the basement and attic.

Are you interested in cars? He asks. Yes, I say. Come and have a look at these. We go down a flight of stairs, into the basement to a garage, Axminister carpet on the floor and fully heated, these are dad's babies. He pulls the first cover off to reveal a 1969 E-TYPE Jaguar, it is dark blue in perfect, well showroom condition, with only 41,000 miles on the clock, totally stunning. What is it worth? I'm not 100% sure but around £100,000. Then he takes the cover off the other one, it is a 1937 Rolls Royce, again perfect condition, one of only 500 ever made. It is number 133, this one is valued at half a million.

I am in heaven, what more could you ask for, I could fleece this guy and he wouldn't even notice, what an opportunity. As I said earlier, I don't even have to look, it falls at my feet. Apparently, his father is partner of an Import and Export Company and spends most of his time abroad, music to my ears, this just gets better and better. We drink Malt whiskey and blow ourselves to bits on coke. The malt was very old and belonged to his dad, but who cares, that's me all over. If I want it, I have it. We spent, let's say, a very intimate night together, definitely one I won't forget in a hurry.

The next morning, it is Saturday or at least I think it is. I'm seeing double and stink of booze. Roddy is much the same, three or four black coffees and still no better. We swop numbers and part company. I said I would call him tonight when my meeting is finished.

I am sure mother said she was at work today, but I cannot go back, not in this state, I am a total mess. Still staggering, I find a café. The biggest full English and more coffee, hoping this might do the trick. The last 12 hours have really got my devious little brain in gear. I somehow remember the alarm code for the house in Chelsea, 7640, god knows how. But it is a good start. I am not after a quick steal and run this time and patience is required. I call Charles to collect me at mid-day to return to Wrenslade.

On my way back, I can see Charles looking at me in the mirror, I know what he is thinking. I just hope I can keep this breakfast down. I always over cook it, one way or another, drink, drugs, greediness, is this because of my childhood, having nothing. It appears now, get the drink down you, get the drugs down you, eat everything on your plate, so no one can take it. off you. But then I always leave a healthy tip, doesn't make sense does it.

The flat is empty apart from Barney, he growls at me, but he will get used to me, I fall on my bed, last night really took it out of me, it was close to madness, I'm wrecked. I must have passed out, Barneys yapping, and mother is home, it is just after 6pm. We agree on a takeaway and a bottle of wine, to be honest, I couldn't do anymore at the moment. She asks how my meeting went, yes very well, I'm sure we have the contract. I am hoping she will offer me to stay as long as I like, but it is early days yet.

It is a good location for dipping in and out of town. The old guy George, next door, appears to be a bit nosey for his own good, I will have to keep an eye on him.

My phone rings, six missed calls in 13 minutes, its Roddy, I will keep him waiting and mother says I can stay as long as I wish. This is excellent news, everything seems to be working out nicely.

That night, I am on the web, looking at E Type Jaguars, I would certainly say his dads is worth over £100,000. Maybe, this could be my next venture, I have to be realistic, I steal watches, rings, antiques, cash, a Jaguar may be more than I can deal with. It is now Thursday, I have talked with Roddy, but haven't seen him since Saturday. He is itching for us to meet, I will make him wait, there is no rush.

When mother is at work I sometimes wonder off to The Grapes just to get out, the silence in the flat is deafening. When I am board it is easy to find trouble. The pub is nice enough, very quiet and secluded, which is in my favour. I usually end up in conversation with Ken the Landlord, the hardest thing of all is remembering what I have said, but I am a good liar and very used to it by now. Every now and then I think back to my old scams, I still don't feel any remorse or sorrow. Everybody in this world is out for themselves and that is all I am doing. What a selfish society we live in.

Banks are the worst, greedy bastards, all of them. I have known many people who needed their help and they turned their backs on them, my dad being one. Then a millionaire walks in and they offer him the world and more. I would love to fleece these bastards one day, who knows, if I did pull it off I would give the lot to the homeless people. Reason being, the banks probably had a hand in making them homeless to start with, When the recession hits it is a lot to do with Banks being down right greedy and it is the ordinary man who pays the price. Yes, I think they are on my list. If you do wrong and get caught you, end up being punished one way or another. These lot walk away laughing and pocket a nice big bonus.

As I am in my moaning zone, I flick on the tv to be greeted by four very dirty looking people shouting at each other, with security guards holding them apart and a small guy in the middle of it trying to talk some sense into them. It was something to do with I will prove you are the father. Who the hell would even think of going anywhere near these people, I couldn't even make out what they were screaming at each other. Do people really watch this crap? I came to the conclusion these must be the benefit scroungers the papers are always on about. As far as I can see they need four things, to have their benefits stopped, use condoms to stop them breeding, a job and the most important, a bar of soap. Where on earth do they find these lot? I am astounded, I must talk to mother about this. I felt sorry for the little guy in the middle of it, he is totally wasting his time, they will never change. Like a nasty disease passed through the generations, I am itching just looking at the television, god knows what his studio smells like.

Another issue is who would employ any of them, for once I am lost for words. If ever I saw the presenter I would advise him to let them rip each other apart and do us all a massive favour. Ok you may say, he is one to talk, yes, I have done bad things, but I have never taken a penny from this Country.

Back in the pub at lunch time, Ken and his wife have run this place for the last 13 years and before that he was a tree surgeon. We chat most afternoons away. It's ok, but it is just not me, no disrespect, this is the kind of place people retire to, then die. With thousands stashed I could stay like this for years, but I need more I am not feeling too well at present, I am, either shivering or sweating, joints aching. I decide to stay off the booze and coke for a while, I'm exhausted, this is a sign to put the brakes on for a bit. Maybe, treat this as a detox. I only drink water for the following 3 days, but I didn't feel any better. Now the paranoia is creeping in. I am still very much wanted, I am constantly looking out of the windows, but if anyone knew I was here I would have been busted by now. It has been 5 days now and I still feel rough, sweating hands, shaking, headaches, either I have picked something up or it is the detox, I am not sure which.

My day now consists of talking to Roddy for half an hour in the morning, reading the newspapers, having a sleep at lunch time, maybe look at my laptop. By the time mother returns from work, I am sat at the table, with phone, notepad, pen and my laptop open, so it looks like I have been working. I am sure she is none the wiser. If I am feeling any better I may venture down the pub tomorrow, this place is starting to feel like prison, it is not doing me any good.

The next day mother is off work, I have to get out of here, I'm going mad. Shower and dressed, still not right, but off I go I feel like everyone is watching me, I'm walking faster and faster, as if I am being chased, am I going mad, I have only seen two people walking a dog. Maybe I am just paranoid. Shaky and sweaty, I enter the pub just after 12oclock. It is quiet as always, Kens wife is behind the bar and delivers my large Gin and Tonic, hopefully a couple of these will sort me out. I ask if Ken is in, apparently, he will be back in an hour or so. He appears, and I get him a beer and we have a pleasant chat, I am now on my third double and still not good but feeling better than I did. Do I have to have the booze and drugs every day, am I an addict? Its nearly four and I am slightly merry walking back, for some unknown reason I can hear my dad telling me to stick to what you know, don't chop and change, brick layers lay bricks, mechanics fix cars. I think it was a sign not to complicate things.

Chapter 13

I have spoken to Roddy again and he has invited me down for the weekend, his father is away again. Thank god, at last some excitement, I was going stir crazy here. I love the Jaguar, but it is not for me, what a shame, I am sure something else will appear. I tell my mother I am off to Paris on business and won't be back until Monday. I have got £5,000 on me, at some point I will have a count up what is in my loft. I call Charles to collect me at 4pm, I cannot wait to see him. I am taking some new casual clothes with my jeans, polo shirts, trainers, jumpers, sorry upper-class jumpers are formerly known as pullovers. I am trying to fit in a bit more instead of looking like Lord Snooty.

I get to Roddy's just after 6pm, his dads away until Tuesday, brilliant party time. That night an Indian restaurant and a bar. We are home by midnight, this suits me, having the place to ourselves. I have to be on my guard, when you are out after midnight everyone is high or pissed and that's when trouble flares and that means police. Hopefully, I blend in a bit better, now we are in we can hit the coke and brandy.

It is not long before he starts telling me about his family, his sister is 41 and lives in Manchester with her 10-year-old daughter and husband. They own a large roofing company. His mother and father got divorced, when he was eight, he has only seen her 3 times since. He really doesn't care where she is, he feels like she just abandoned them. Just because her and my dad didn't get on, I feel she punished us for it. My dad did an excellent job of bringing us up, I have got nothing to thank her for, we don't even mention her. I can totally see where he is coming from, I felt that my dad never wanted me and when dickhead Gary moved in, well let's just say twos company, three is a crowd. When I left I never once heard my mother begging me to stay. Some parents do a crap job and get away with it or, so they think, when you are a child you do not forget.

Looking at Roddy he has everything, but I know his mother has damaged him, much like myself. In one way it is time to change the subject, I see he is getting a little upset. What about your family Adam? A very rare opportunity to actually tell the truth for once, if any lies emerge he would be none the wiser. Most of my story is true, with the odd lie thrown in. But as you know I don't reveal many details, if any about myself. This has unlocked a door to a very cold dark room for me, I feel mad more than anything else. But you know the old saying, don't get mad get even. I am going to make my mother pay. She thought I was dead, but still made no effort to find out, when I have finished she will wish I was dead.

Saturday is here, and Roddy wants to see the Star Wars film at the cinema, it is not my cup of tea, but go anyway, just to keep him happy. I get my own way, but this time I haven't, and I am not too pleased about it. I'm finding this film boring, but my mind is full of ideas and future projects.

I have just realised it is mother's birthday on Thursday, what an excellent chance to spoil her. After the film we head off for pizza and some drinks, everywhere is getting very busy very fast. I do not really want to be in the middle of this, I try to talk Roddy into going home, but he won't hear of it. I have started feeling ill again, this makes it even more difficult. He insists on this pizza restaurant, I agree just to keep him happy.

Once inside the only table left is one right in the centre, I really don't like this, but I have no choice, I always go in a corner. We get a bottle of wine and browse the menu, well he is, I am peeking over the top to see who is around. I have made eye contact with a woman and a guy, I look away, but I know they are still looking, this is worrying me, this keeps on for a good 10 minutes. My paranoia is now running a mock, sweat dripping down my face, I am sure they are cops I grab my phone, sorry Rod I have to take this and disappear outside and run. Three or four streets away I grab the first cab, to Camden please, that was close.

Looking out of the back window all seems ok. How am I going to explain to Rod, I haven't got a clue, but I am sure something will come up. The driver stops outside the Seven Stars pub, I pay him and stand outside. I have got eight missed calls and just don't know what to do next, now that is not like me. The scary thing is I am always on my guard and this evening could have ended in tragedy. I have been stood here a good 15 minutes and I am still gasping for air. I think the last x amount of years has really taken its toll on me. Finally, I call Rod back and tell him the reason I ran was there was a guy in there I had had a run in with a couple of years ago and just panicked. It stemmed from a property deal that went very wrong. I am not sure if he swallowed it or not, but it was the best I could come up with. We arrange to meet back at his, I love the chase, but this is getting a bit too close for comfort. Perhaps my mother's is a safe option, perhaps they were not police, but I certainly wasn't going to hang around to find out.

Back at Rods, now I am still beating myself up, how stupid was I, I'm playing with fire, I know I am going to get burnt at some point. In one way it is better to get caught with lots of cash, than lots of drugs. You will stand a greater chance of a more lenient sentence, I must stay away from the centre of town from now on.

I spend the next couple of hours just spinning out lie after lie. Usually, I can read people very well, but I still don't know if he believes me. My old habit of peering out of windows has also returned I will have to stop it, that is a sign something is wrong. We crash out at 2am, full of coke and booze, but I am still struggling to sleep, my veins feel like the underground with trains racing through one after the other.

Sunday morning, I am in a shit state, with a capital S, shivering, shaking, I feel like I am going to blow. Rod invites me to stay again tonight, I am not sure I want to, I crave the safety of Mothers flat, he keeps on and on until I finally give in, he wants to go out again, but I insist only if we stay local. Sometimes it is easier to do it rather than trying to get out of it. There is a bit of an atmosphere between us today, maybe a lover's tiff, hopefully, it will pass as the day goes on. I do love London compared to Doncaster, it is like Vegas, but every time I step on the pavement, I know it could be my last, there are Police sirens every five minutes here, that makes me jumpy, on its own. I wonder how much I have actually netted since I started, I can't even think straight, let alone add up, it must be over a million, I would be a bit disappointed if it was any less Having people call me Sir and even Lord, but what a train crash really, constantly on the run, on my own. But every cloud, it was tax free.

Sunday night is nice and quiet, we arrive back before 9pm, just merry. I think I will seize the chance to drop a rohypnol in his drink. I'm chomping at the bit to have a proper look around here. It is just before 11pm and Rod is out cold, when he wakes I will blame it on a new supply of coke. Right coast clear, let's get searching. I probably have an hour, so best get cracking.

All the bedrooms only unearth a small amount of jewellery, nothing worth taking, a bit disappointing so far. From experience I know anything worth taking would be well buried. so next stop look in on Rod, still out of it. Now his father's office, this could be interesting One thing I hate is a wasted journey, if I put the effort in I like a reward at the end of it. Into the office, there are filing cabinets each side of an old green leather top desk. There are some jackets hanging behind the door, I sift through them first I find two twenty-pound notes in one and nothing in the other two, so £40 up, not a bad start.

The filing cabinets are all locked and I cannot find a safe anywhere, I am sure he would have one. Now to the desk, all the draws are open, this could be a gold mine, I hope. There is a cheque attached to an invoice for plumbing work, so there must be a cheque book somewhere nearby. I know these desks from old, lots of hidden compartments and sliding panels. I open a hidden draw to find a cheque book and also an envelope containing some very graphic photos of, I take it it must be his father, with a young boy. I feel sick the boy must be only 5 or 6. I cannot even bring myself to explain to you how disgusting it is. They look quite old, maybe early 80's, flowery wall paper and dodgy hair styles.

I place the cheque book back, but these photos could prove to be priceless. I take one last look, the boy in them, is it rod? I am quite sure it is not, but people change, I don't look anything like what I was, thank god. I have only heard of stuff like this when you see it first hand, it is frightening. Memories of the scout camp have just returned. There are 7 pictures all together and now in my inside pocket of my jacket. I seriously just want out of here now, I know I cannot run tonight but asap in the morning. I am very tormented by this, being abused myself I know exactly what that poor boy went through.

I don't agree with capital punishment however, if it were to return just for these monsters I would be all for it. Now how much are these pictures worth, I think £10,000 each, I cannot see why not, I would get £70,000 and he would get his pictures back or I could just send them to the police with his name and address. I think I am sure I know what he will choose. The next step is how to approach it, I have never met him before, I will try the friendly, honest, helpful friend act first and see where that gets me. It always worked well befriending someone, Stuart is a classic example. I think I may have just discovered a way possibly to find out if it is him.

In the study there is a glass cabinet with I am sure a stack of photo albums in. When the time is right I will bring up the old days and see if Rod will show me any snaps, it is worth a try.

It is now Monday morning and Rods a little worse for wear, he actually looks a strange shade of green, he decides to phone in sick apparently, that is the first time ever, that proves what a bad influence I am. Many black coffees and I say there are no pictures of your sister in here, come to think of it there are none of you either. His dad doesn't like to put pictures on the wall unless it is by a well-known artist. So, you don't have any then? Yes, of course, Adam go in the study, there is a glass cabinet with photo albums in, can you fetch them, and we will have a look.

We sit next to each other and one at a time start to look. The first two, the pictures are mostly black and white, very old, then onto another, he points out different relations, but it is still not what I need. Then a lovely one of his dad stood next to an old Mercedes, Rod says that's my dad and he vaguely remembers the car. Yes, 100% it is the same man who is abusing the boy. We carry on looking, now into another book, a photo of Rod's 7th Birthday party, Rod is in the middle, just about to blow his candles out. His mum and dad are stood behind him, his sister to his right and the boy is sat on his left. Oh, what a lovely photo, who is the boy? That is Simon, he lived next door to us in Chiswick. Do you ever see him? No, it is very sad, when he was 10 he contacted Leukaemia, he only lasted not even a year, he died just before his 11th birthday. I can feel myself filling up, what a horrible time that poor boy had. It was only a year or two later that his parents moved. My dad thinks they went somewhere in Cumbria.

We were all devastated, he was a lovely kid, my best friend, we had a great time. I used to stay at his house and he would stay at ours, as much as anything, he was like the brother I never had. I must get my hands on this picture, when Rod goes to shower I will put them back and swipe it then. It is astonishing how you can unearth such a horrific and very sad tale in such a short space of time. Looking at the Birthday picture it all blends in the furniture, carpet, wallpaper. I am sure Simon was abused at the age of 6 or 7 and I bet it was during these sleepovers. I feel appalled trying to profit from this, I cannot help Simon, but I can hit this bastard where it hurts. These sort only care about money and status. From what I can gather he is a very forceful man, someone, maybe, not to be messed with, it is his way or no way, that's the impression I get. Well all I can say is he hasn't met me yet. Rod is in the shower and the photo is in the envelope with the others, a nice job if I say so myself.

Was this the reason why his mother left? Did she know what was going on? Did he abuse her as well? Perhaps she was so frightened of him, she had no choice but to leave. I always felt sorry for myself, the rubbish upbringing, crap schools, but now I realise, perhaps I had it easy compared to others. I have spent years saying poor old me, there is always someone worse off than yourself I guess Simon would have been a couple of years younger than me. After all the trauma he went through, the poor lad is maybe better off where he is. Abuse and illness is certain to destroy the strongest of souls.

This brings back memories of the Scout Group, I try to put the lid on it but occasionally it creeps up behind me. The one thing that will hurt this man more than anything is knowing that he has been found out. Simon, I promise you I will do my utmost best.

It is late morning and Charles collects me and I return to mothers. I class myself as well travelled and thick skinned, but this has really shaken me, I am actually dreading coming face to face with him. Mother comes in just after 6pm and for her birthday I am paying for her and a friend to spend the day in London, also throwing in £1000 to spend, she is ecstatic to say the least. I arrange a local taxi for their trip. Charles is very good, but I don't want her knowing where I have been most weekends. Most of all, I feel sorry for Rod, having a father like that. The situation has changed everything, Rod is a great guy but now I feel he is just a passenger on my bus, he will be dropped off at the relevant stop. Mother cannot thank me enough but believe me the pleasure is definitely all mine.

One thing I would pay to see is his face when he realises his beloved photos are missing. I am just having an easy week here, the photos are in the loft, safely tucked away. Most evenings I am at the table with my laptop open. I am pretending to be working, putting together a property deal, even talking to myself on the phone. So, my stake would be £850,000, mothers ears prick up. Ok I may be a little short, I am very interested, give me a little more time to sort the cash out and this is due to start the middle of March? Ok, leave it with me, thanks, bye. This has definitely caught her interest. Everything alright Adam? Yes, well I hope so, we are building some luxury flats in Battersea and I am £50,000 short on my stake. I have £800,000, I have to find £50,000. I am owed some favours, hopefully, I will be alright. When do you need it by? Well within the next two weeks really. How many flats are you building? 10 all together, with the starting price of 1.1 million. I have planted the seed, lets see how it grows.

Whilst I am on I see another story, fraudster gives police the slip in Pizza Restaurant, I was right then, bloody hell that was close. Another picture of me is not good. I find it a little funny really that these cops couldn't catch a cold, let alone me.

Chapter 14

Thursday is here, and my mother and her friend are both off to town, this gives me the chance to think and sort out what is next. I am off to Rods again on Friday, hopefully, his father will be in, I am looking forward to it. It is nearly 1 o'clock, nothing much is happening, I think I will slip off to the Grapes. Just had a horrendous nose bleed, ten minutes later it has stopped, this isn't right, I know something is wrong, but what I don't know is what. Anyway, to the pub I go. It is nearly empty, only Ken and two old boys sat the other side of the bar. Large Gin and Tonic, after a short while Ken sits with me and just the usual chit chat. The two old boys have just left, so it is just the two of us.

Then out of nowhere he says, I know who you are and places a newspaper cutting in front of me. I strongly deny the accusation, I do not know what you mean. Listen, don't take me for a fool, I am not as stupid as you think, are you seriously telling me that is not you? Well, that is it, game over, my reign of terror is finally at an end. Then he places his hand on my knee, under the table and says your secret is safe with me, we just have to be nice to each other. I now perfectly understand exactly what he wants. If he was going to rat on me he would have done it before now. One thing I know I am not running again, well not for now anyway, there is too much cash on offer. If I can rob Rods dad and my mother I will disappear abroad and be very nicely set up, so for now I agree and bide my time. I know I am cornered, so my only option is to come out fighting or I could stab him and make it look like a burglary gone wrong, but that is not my style.

His wife leaves for the shops, I drink up ready to depart, he is having none of it. Where, do you think you are going? Home. No, you are not, get upstairs, he locks the doors, come on. He chose the bathroom, the next 10 minutes were revolting, to put it politely. It is certainly not the first time I have done it, but what can I do. One saving grace is when you mess with me you will suffer, that is guaranteed, you fat smelly slob.

I ask him where I can get coke, he has a contact. I want £500 worth, he says he will have it tomorrow, I leave him my number and he will text me. Back to the flat, I am a bit worse for wear. I have let myself down, one of my rules was to always expect the unexpected and I have let this pig get the better of me, well not for long.

Mother returns, full of champagne and shopping bags, they had a wonderful time. She has a few hundred left and offers it back to me, but I point blank refuse. The only good thing that has emerged from this awful day is I have got top Brownie points. The sun is shining bright from my arse, what a sneaky sod I am. I am just waiting for a nice pay-out, shouldn't be long now.

I collect my gear from Ken, no favours today his wife is here, but I fancy a few drinks. I cannot be seen to be avoiding him, it is best to keep him on my side. I know for a fact when he has had his fun he will grass me anyway and pocket a nice reward, or so he thinks. I have been in this game many years, fraud, theft, blackmail, you name it, the one thing I know for certain is, I am better at it than him.

Mother keeps on at me to visit a doctor, but that is out of the question, I do feel very ill, I just say, I am over worked, sitting in a doctors waiting room I may as well have a target on my back. I am taking 10 to 14 pain killers a day, just to function, but as you know, mixed with coke and booze, it really isn't a good idea. Also, I have a rash on my legs and chest, typing my symptoms in, it could be anything. Anyway, struggling a bit, but it is Friday and I am off to Rods. I have to ask Charles to pull into a layby, I feel sick and have horrible stomach ache, he offers to take me back, but I will just keep going, these days I am not someone who just gives up and I am dying to get a look at his father.

I arrive at Rods at around 5pm, apparently his dad will be back tomorrow, but it is cool for me to stay. Are you ok Adam, you don't look good? Yes fine, just too many late nights and over worked. God do I really look that bad, perhaps more makeup will really do the trick. There is now a large amount of cash in the loft, also photos, I wonder if it is worth getting a safe deposit box, but they are probably safer where they are.

I am getting a little concerned about my health and this rash appears to be rifer by the day. Seeing a doctor is not an option. It could even be HIV or something or nothing. As far as being intimate with Rod, I will just have to swerve it, any excuse will do, he is the last person I want to be affected. But, the nastiness in me says by all means let Ken have it. How did I get to this, I was brought up to be truthful and honest, now look at the mess I am in. I got myself into it and so I will get myself out of it. Rod is even pressuring me to see a doctor, in the, end I agree, but not yet, at least that shuts him up for now.

We have a very chilled evening in, he cooks a bolognaise and have a couple of glasses of wine, to be honest I feel so grotty, there is no way I was able to go out. Saturday morning and I ask what time is your dad home? Between 2pm and 3pm, great I cannot wait. I am not going to mess about, I am going straight for the kill, when the time is right. If I get the £70,000 I have decided to disappear for a couple of weeks. In total, with what I have got and if I can squeeze the £50,000 out of mother, at a rough guess I should have close to £180,000. Now I can see myself lying on a lovely beach, sipping Champers. It is all within reach, just be patient and don't take any unnecessary risks.

His dad is home early, just after lunch, straight away, yes, it is him. We introduce and shake hands. He wants to take us to a restaurant tonight, I am not keen, but I want to find out what makes him tick. I cannot take my eyes off him, he even looks like a nasty piece of work. The word I am looking for is maybe ruthless. The thing is I am here until Sunday, so I do not really want to upset him quite yet, maybe tomorrow. At 7 o'clock we all head into town to a Tai Restaurant. I insist on a corner table, somehow, I think they were wondering why.

After the Pizza do I am more than nervous, but I have no choice but to sit it out. Our meal is faultless and to be fair, it was a very pleasant evening. If you didn't know what he had done, he comes across as a really nice guy. He is good for the cash, just his watch and rings must be £20,000 alone But I am not going to be greedy, well there is a first time for everything I suppose. £70,000 will do. Before I leave tomorrow, I will drop the bomb. He seems to want to know a lot about me, but I am not giving anything away, that is certainly one thing I am really good at.

For once we have an early night, if you call 12.30 early. Before bed he said I was welcome to stay as long as I like. After I have got my money I may take him up on that. How Kind. Elevenish the next morning and I am ready for the off. My car arrives at 11.30am, Rod is upstairs, his father is in his office. I find a piece of paper and write my mobile number, also call me regarding abuse photos. As I hear Rod coming down stairs I dart in and chuck it on his desk. I bid everybody farewell and I am gone. I wonder how and what is going through his mind.

Mother is home and informs me that I have a doctor's appointment on Tuesday at 11.30am, I really do not want this but I do know that I have to attend. Mother is also interested to see if I have managed to raise the other £50,000, all I say is I am still waiting for a decision and leave it at that, now I can tell she is really interested.

That evening browsing the web, a story has appeared, some guy in Kent says I was lodging with him and ran off with his life savings of £55,000. I have no idea who he is, I have never been to Kent in my life. Perhaps, there are two of me, what a cheek. It is fine taking the blame for something I have done but that is definitely nothing to do with me.

Tuesday morning is here and off to see Doctor Stephens, trying to hide the best I can in the waiting room. It is nearly empty, lucky for me. So, in I go, I may as well be truthful, the nose bleeds, feeling very tired and weak, I show him the rash, I also tell him I am homosexual. I am actually straight down the line with him, it is actually a very nice feeling for once. I don't have a regular partner, I have had many over the last 16 years. I also use about £150.00 of cocaine per week. Dr Stephens takes some blood, gives me some cream for the rash and wants to see me again this time next week. I ask him, what do you think it is? But he is not saying, lets see what the blood tests come back with. Oh, and until we know don't have any sexual contact with anyone. Well, I think what he really meant was don't have any sexual contact with anyone other than Ken.

My left arm is hurting from giving blood. I call Rod to cancel next weekend. I just bullshit him saying I am away on business. I must confess, I am getting worried, Dr Stephens face said it all. But what is the point in waiting until I know the results. I told mother the doctor said it was a virus that has been going around. Just take it easy and rest.

Still no calls from Rods dad, I will let him stew. I stay in nearly all week, sleeping, listening to music, how boring, the days drag, absolute boredom. How some people do this day in day out is beyond me. Then again, they may wonder what makes me tick. Years ago, it excited me, the con, the chase and away. I am not so sure now. If I need any hospital treatment I know I will be caught within minutes and if I don't I will end up dead probably in a hotel room. A bit the same as the rich and famous.

On Thursday night I get a text from Ken, reading come tomorrow between two and four, she is going out. I reply, ok see you then. There is something in that bathroom I want to check out, it caught my eye last time. I despise the bloke, but I may have a plan. I get to the pub around 1.30pm, it is very quiet. Ken greats me with a gin and tonic, then sits with me. Can you get me £2000 of coke? Yeah, no problem. It is not for me, it is a gift for a friend. I need some time. What about

100

this time next week, I will bring the cash with me. Great that is sorted. Now his wife has gone the pub is empty. So up to the bathroom, I entre first and undress. As I thought the bath panel is very loose, I can get my hand behind it. After this disgusting ordeal, back to the bar for a drink, he really doesn't know what is going to hit him, plus he could have picked up anything from me. I am definitely winning this battle.

Only a couple of days till I see the doctor. If it is bad news I have only got myself to blame. People would say serves him bloody right. The big question is where and who did I get it from. I must have been with at least 50 or 60 different people over the years, it could have been anyone. Still no call from Rods dad. Finally, back to the doctors, that week seemed like a year. Come in take a seat, well it is not good news Adam you have Hepatitis B, also your liver is damaged, and your kidneys are not working properly. I have referred you to St Pauls hospital, you should get an appointment in the next couple of weeks. I thought I had HIV? No, this is not good, you need to change your lifestyle and get regular treatment. What happens if I don't have treatment? You will almost certainly be dead within two years. I leave the surgery and don't know what to do, for once I am stuffed, if I do and stuffed if I don't. The only good thing is I am not HIV positive. So, it is possible I will be dead before I am 40.

I know I have to change, stop the coke and booze. But it is all I know, to me they are my friends, what would I do without them? He wants to see me again in 4 weeks, I don't even know if I will still be here, I may have moved on by then. There is no way I can sit in this flat for 4 weeks, 1 week was bad enough, that would send me over the edge. I always thought if nothing is happening, make something happen. When people sit idol that is usually when trouble comes calling. I am also finding it difficult lying to mother constantly. I wish she could stop with the questions, she is starting to piss me off. I have got enough on my mind without her going on. Another pain in the ass is I must catch the post when my appointment arrives. I don't want her seeing it, that would be more interrogation. This is all getting a bit messy for my liking, I feel like I am in a washing machine going around and around and around. I need to move on for a while. I cannot help thinking I am near my sell by date, everybody has their day, but I am not giving up.

I finally receive a call from Rod's dad, I take it in my room, with the door shut. What do you want? £70,000. How did you get them? It doesn't matter, I also have the photo of Rods 7th birthday, the one with Simon sat next to him when he was blowing the candles out. OK, OK, where and when. Right, Thursday afternoon 2 o'clock in the car park opposite The Yew Tree Pub on Brighton sea front I look forward to seeing you. So perhaps, everything's falling into place, meet him Thursday, collect my cash, then Friday Ken should have the gear, I am still waiting for my mother to make me an offer. My plan is, when I get the £70,000 to disappear for a week or so he doesn't really have any choice in the matter.

I think I will go to Brighton early on Thursday, I know the yew tree is right opposite the car park, so that would make a good look out point. I will also use taxis not Charles, I want to keep this one under wraps, for all I know it could be a set up, but then again, I will have photos on me, so that is probably not in his best interest. We would both end up nicked and he would probably get longer than me, so I am actually in a very comfortable position.

Mother is really starting to do my head in. I cannot wait to get away. I have told her I am off to Norfolk on business for a week or so. She has just told me she would like to invest but can only raise £40,000. I tell her it is a very sound deal with an excellent return, but I would need it in cash. She promises me she will have it within a week. Now it is all falling into place. I think £40,000 is justified for my crap childhood. Once all of the cash is in I will be gone within the hour. It is more than enough for a new start.

Thursday is soon here, and it is party time. I just have a gut feeling this guy is not going to give up without a fight. I have booked a local taxi for midday and dress casually, no unwanted attention today, I always want to be the main event, but not today. I am suffering today, I ache all over and get the odd dizzy spell. The rash has also spread, diarrhoea, headaches, but I am nearly there.

The taxi drops me just around the corner from the pub, perhaps I got here a little too early, but I am here now. A large gin and tonic and I take a window seat, with a newspaper, I have a perfect view, the main thing is he is on his own. Just a waiting game now.

On the net last night and now there is loads of stories about me. One that sticks out is a guy claims I rented his house in Suffolk, bounced a cheque on him and trashed the place before I left. It is news to me and now my offences are over a 100. The Police would really love to have a chat, but I 'am a bit busy at present. I hate being blamed for something I haven't done. When I am done and dusted I am thinking of America, it is a huge target and they do love us Brits, I quite fancy it, I have never been and there is plenty for me. Yes, I may do some research, the UK has been good to me, but I have exhausted it now.

This pub is reasonably busy, a good thing in one way and not in another. It is after two and I am fixated on the car park. I don't know if he will be in a car or on foot, so I will let him get there first and he will almost certainly call me. I am getting a bit edgy, it is nearly 3pm and still nothing. I just have to sit tight, then he calls. Where are you? Have you got my pictures? Yes, do you have the cash? Yeah, I am by the parking machine. I will be there in five minutes. I can see him, and he is alone with a small blue rucksack. I drink up and go for the kill. As I approach, I can see he is not very happy. I just want this done and away. We lean on the railings looking out to sea. Who are you? Just a friend of Rods, I will give you this on two conditions, one you stay away from Rod and two I never want to clap eyes on you again. I pass him the envelope and he gave me the rucksack, that was all that was said. Now a fast get away, back to mothers.

I am delighted, what a result, I should do this for a living. Into a cab and gone. I will have to count up when I am back, I unzip the top of the bag and it is full of cash. Perhaps I should have demanded more but I am happy. Back to mothers and I am walking up the stairs, George appears, oh hello Adam, have you got a minute to chat? Yes, of course. I go into his flat, god it is smelly, that old musty smell. He offers me a cup of tea, but I decline, so what can I do for you George? Well I have been talking with your mother and she informs me of an investment opportunity in Battersea. I was wondering if I could put some in? Yes, of course, you will double your money within 12 months. Well, it is sat in the bank doing nothing, I might as well make something. How much are you looking at, is £30,000 enough? Yes, definitely, the only thing is I would need it in cash, this time next week and at the same time I will give you a contract. Ok, son. I am going away tomorrow, but I will be back by next weekend.

Back in the flat I cannot believe it, walking up the stairs and getting given £30,000. It is not right taking the old boy's savings, but he offered, I didn't ask, I don't care who I get it off. In my business you get what you can and run onto the next victim. What do they say, there is no fool like an old fool, so better I have it, you couldn't even make it up. Can I honestly take his savings? Yes, why not, silly old fool. Next weekend I should have in the region of £200,000, now that is music to my ears.

That evening I explain my conversation with George to Mother and she is all for it. Lying in bed, I cannot sleep, it is ridiculous, how easy it's been. It is harder taking sweets from a kid. I am firmly in the driving seat, I am so looking forward to a week away, on my own and relax. I ordered some stronger pain killers off the internet, paid with a dud card of course, hopefully these should see me alright. A taxi booked for 10.30 the next morning. I owe Charles some money, so I doubt if I will use him again. I spotted a nice hotel in Essex not too far from here, but far enough. For some reason a lot of people I have come across are running through my mind, some of which I would like to see again but I know that is a nonstarter.

Friday morning and Rod is on the phone asking if I want to stay the weekend. I kindly decline, saying I am away but next weekend sounds good. My belongings are packed into 3 holdalls, not much to show for all these years, mostly clothes and shoes, shameful really. I must have stolen at least 40 Rolex watches in the past, just the cash from them alone would be thousands. I have got £30,000 on me, the rest is in the loft, in the blue rucksack tucked away nicely.

Chapter 15

My cabs here, the coast looks clear outside and I am off. This hotel in Basildon looks very nice, I desperately need a break, every day goes by I am feeling worse but hopefully these new tablets will do the trick. I am trying to make a deal with myself to slow up, but I am not sure I can. Once I am in Essex I will drop this phone and buy another. The driver introduces himself as John, where to sir? The Spread Eagle Hotel, Marshall Street, Basildon and give him the postcode. When he drops me off I will go in but not stay, too cover my tracks. Just in case anyone asks any questions, I sit in the back slumped down behind the passenger seat. Last thing I want is any attention.

I have £30,000 on me plus a bag of coke and a Rolex I found in the bottom of my bag. Forgot I had it, a nice little bonus. We have only been on the road for about 40 minutes and there seems to be something wrong with the car. I think we may have a puncture. Sir, I will have to pull over, he pulls onto the hard shoulder and jumps out. The tyre behind me is flat. I'm sorry sir I will have to ask you to get out, I have to jack up the car. Great, just what I don't need, me standing at the side of a busy duel carriage way for the whole world to see. John places my bags by the side of the car, this is a terrible situation, I am at his mercy and well and truly stuck. I am stood on the grass verge with my back to the oncoming traffic, trying to hide as much as possible. It only took him 10 minutes or so to change the wheel, but it felt like a life time You can get back in now Sir, sorry for the delay, he is placing my bags back in the boot.

I hear him talking to someone, as I look around a police car has stopped behind us, shit it is all over. Pretending to look at my phone I just froze, that is me finished, but just keep calm, John gets back in. What did they want? Oh, just checking we were alright. Few my heart was racing, bloody hell, talk about a close shave, funny in one way, I was right, there for the taking and they still missed me. John informs me that we are 20 minutes away. When I get there, I think I need to take stock of the situation, things have got slightly messy, I feel like I am snatching at things without thinking. I see people out with their kids and couples together, I know I am missing out, but I am trapped in this nasty little world of lying, cheating and stealing, sometimes maybe it would be for the best if I were caught. But I am a spineless little rat, so I choose to keep running.

We pull up outside the hotel, it is very busy, I pay John with a nice tip and he disappears. I don't go into the Spread Eagle, I start to walk, I don't know this area, but it is much quieter away from the town centre, I will just see where I end up. I find The Crazy Bear Hotel and restaurant, a much quieter location. I prefer this, I enter and book in for 5 nights. It is a very nice double room, it is £85.00 a night, including breakfast. I am on the second floor, a young lady called Sam shows me to my room, it is not up with London establishments, but at £85 a night I don't expect it to be. It is all I need for now, living with Mother is very hard work.

I now have a little freedom my room looks out onto the main road, thank god. I can keep a look out, by the way my paranoia is rife when it starts. Every siren or someone shouting I am up at the window, I know it is pointless, but I cannot seem to help myself. I settle in, food and drink in the room, it is only 7.20pm, I fancy some action. Within minutes I find a visiting masseur on line, based in Essex with discretion assured. You know the sort I mean with extras if required. I book him for 9 o'clock, all my requirements are, a tanned, muscular, male between 25 and 35. It is money up front and his name is Mark. I have always fancied a go at this, but never followed it through, why not you only live once.

Feeling so ill over the past few weeks I am hoping this will give me the lift I need. I feel like I am living on my nerves at present, coke and booze calms me, I hope this will too. Five to nine and a tap on my door, even that tap makes me jump, who is there? It's Mark. Oh, come in. Well he makes the Chippendales look like dustmen, my word he is stunning, six-foot, short blonde hair, blue eyes and packed with muscle, dressed

110

to perfection. God, I wish he was mine, I don't make a habit of drooling, but this time I just cannot help myself.

It is £300.00 for two hours, that is for a full massage, and the whole package, if you get my drift. The first 10 minutes or so we just chat, with a glass of champagne, then to business. Wow, why haven't I done this before, it certainly beats any drugs I have ever had and definitely the best £300.00 I have ever spent. For a little while the guilt stepped in, thinking of Roddy, the only thing that made me feel better about this is that I know it won't last. Mark leaves just after 11pm and I say I will be asking for him next time, I hope there is a next time.

Mother has left me a voicemail saying George and herself will have the cash by no later than Friday. I am having doubts as to whether I can do this, rip off your own mother and a pensioner. But one thing I don't do is pick and choose. I spend the next couple of hours drinking and snorting, glued to the window, what a great night, I know I will suffer tomorrow. One shocking thought is that I do not remember the last time I went more than a week without a drink or drugs, it must have been when I lived with Aunt Ruby.

The next morning, I call mother back and everything is on track. She also informs me that Dr Stephens has been trying to get hold of me and can I call him as soon as possible. This has got me worried, what possibly could he want. The only way to find out is call him, but not yet. I have decided to keep my phone for now, but it is time to go for a wonder, I had enough of staying in at mothers, so just casual dress is the order and off I go. Just the usual shops, nothing different, then I see a chap sweeping outside a club called Room 500. I say, what is the place like? It is buzzing every night, tonight is 80s night, always good, do you fancy it? Yes, why not? He disappears inside and returns with two free entry passes. I am Andy, I introduce myself as Paul. Doors open at 7.30pm, hope to see you then. Yes, I will give it a go, why not.

The rest of the day I sit in a couple of bars, killing time, I do enjoy my own company half the time. Returning to the hotel around 5pm and decide to try the restaurant, it is very good, only half full. I don't know if there is a fire station nearby, but you can hear a lot of sirens, that really puts me on edge. I am feeling awful, weak and extremely tired. I retreat to my room for some sleep, it could be a late night. I am used to high profile functions, blagging my way in, now I am attending an 80's night, I still have the snob in me.

I wonder what the doctor wants, could it be a set up, I may call him tomorrow. After some sleep, shower and down to the bar, a couple of drinks to straighten up. I head off to the club, I am in two minds about this but, I am on my way. If it is crap I will just leave. Only a short walk and I am struggling with that. Inside it is already busy and loud. A bottle of Champagne and into the corner. Once people spot the Champagne it is not long, and they are with you, generally, it is the best magnet you get. Within seconds two girls and a guy are right next to me, all of which look like mid to late twenty's. They introduce themselves as Paula, Sharon and Kev. I'm John, it is the first name that came into my head. Sharon and Kev say they work for an Engineering firm the other side of town and Paula tells me she is an office worker, they ask what do you do John? I am part of a Racing team based in Paris I don't know the first thing about Motor Racing, but it sounded good at the time. We only started last year. I am here on business for a week, I see the overwhelming delight on their faces, as they've just found a rich friend. I buy a couple more bottles, which we share. Very generous of me, in one way. It is getting way to busy in here for my liking.

Just thinking of planning my escape, Sharon and Kev are getting ready to leave, I didn't realise they were a couple. They thank me for the drinks and leave. So now it is Paula and myself. What are you doing Paula? I think I will stay for a while, she seems a really nice girl, I don't want to leave her alone. Have you eaten? No. Do you fancy an Indian? Yes, that would be lovely. You will have to direct me as I am a stranger round here. We enter the Bengal Palace, apparently it is the best in town. It is nice and quiet, I am just glad to be out of the club.

As always, I like to find out information about other people rather than them knowing too much about me. I order the drinks, a vodka and coke for the lady and a gin and tonic for myself, thank you. You are very posh, we are not used to that around here. Well, I come from a millionaire back round, all of my family are millionaires and high flyers. My father is the managing Director of shell Oil Company, my mother has her own on-line fashion business and my brother just swans about in Morocco, living it up. Are you a millionaire? Yes, of course. And you are staying at the Bear? My PA is on leave and it was very short notice. Its fine, usually I am either in Paris or London. Paula was fixed on my every word, I love a good story, how someone falls for it.

I'm 35 now how old are you, oh, I am very sorry, how rude, I do apologise. No, no, it is ok, I am 33. I thought you were only 26 or 27, a compliment can go a long way. You are charming and generous. No problem, the pleasure is all mine, actually she has been very good company. I am not used to females, but I really like her, she is slim, good looking, with dark shoulder length hair. Straight away you can see she looks after herself. She has not long been out of a 4 year relationship and now shares a small house with her friend. Are you married or with anyone John? No, no I don't have the time. Surely someone like you must have someone? There was someone years ago but unfortunately, she passed away suddenly. Oh, I am sorry. No, it is fine, it was a long time ago now.

For the life of me I cannot figure out what I am doing with her, I am a gay male with illness, wanted by the Police. Maybe, I am lonely, I have really clicked with her, actually, I fancy her, but it just cannot happen. One thing I cannot have is passengers and secondly the last woman I was with was Gwen and that was years ago. No, I think this will stay as a friendship, it is the only way. We are the last in the restaurant and we swop numbers. I insist on getting her a cab and paying. I will not have you walking home at this time of night. We part company and arrange to meet for lunch the following day at 12pm. Paula says she is owed some holiday by her firm, so it is not a problem, I am looking forward to it. The next morning I book a chauffeur driven Mercedes for 1 o'clock, to take us to a Michelin star restaurant called The Blue Goose, I would like to treat her.

Roddy has called and wants to know if I am still on for the weekend and he is missing me, I miss him to, little does he know I am having a whale of a time with his father's money. I promise I will see him next weekend. I also contact Dr Stephens, he would like to see me as soon as possible. He can wait, I know I am ill, so what is new.

Paula arrives before 12pm and we grab a quick drink in the bar, before the car arrives. So where are you taking me then? Be patient, you will have to wait and see. The car arrives, and I make him wait, just because I can. I keep him outside for twenty minutes, I am an awkward little twat, when I want to be. We will come out when we are ready. The arrogance in me is shining through. I'm the king of the Castle, number 1, you will do as I say, this is where I want to be. The driver doesn't look very happy to have been kept waiting, but so what, this is more like how I used to be, very demanding and rude.

Within 30 or 40 minutes we arrive at the restaurant. Paula's face is glowing. This will cost a fortune. Don't even think of it, just enjoy. I have never been anywhere like this before, film stars come here and people off the television. Just relax, you are with me. I tell the driver to wait, I don't know how long we will be. My wallet is stuffed with cash, so I am in charge. I made a point of telling him and not asking him, extremely rude but I am the boss today.

I have got £4500.00 with me, that should be sufficient. This is very exclusive, just the vehicles outside run into millions. I am really lording it up, I even snap my fingers for the waiter, they just cannot do enough for you, not bad at all for a no mark kid from Doncaster. In one way it is a rag to riches story, just not in the usual way it is done. The nasty snob in me is well and truly out, I even give Paula lessons on how to use the cutlery. The food is divine, faultless, with champagne on top what more could you ask for.

Most of the conversation is centred around Paula, whenever it heads my way I just divert it and change the subject. Paula has been an office supervisor for an Insurance Company for 7 years, her parents moved to Great Yarmouth four years ago to retire by the sea. She has also lived in Essex all her life. So how did you get on at school? It was awful, as soon as I could leave I did, I hated the teachers, they were worse than useless, I don't know how they had the front to call themselves teachers. I only had two real friends, well that was two more than me, Lucy and Poppy. Poppy moved to France with her parents, must be 8-9 years ago. We talk once or twice a year, but people move on don't they. Yeah, I know all about that.

So what happened to Lucy? There is a slight pause, she went clubbing one Friday night in Luton, she had a boyfriend there. In the early hours they had an argument and she walked off to get a taxi. I was staying in Yarmouth at the time, it was about 2 in the morning, she got out of the cab and was hit by a van, she suffered serious head and back injuries and died the next morning, she was only 25. Oh, I am so sorry, I didn't mean to upset you. It was a terrible sad time, to make things worse the driver was 3 times over the limit. The trial lasted 8 days and he only got 6 years and usually you only serve 3. There was an appeal, but nothing changed, my friend's life was only worth 3 years!

I am sorry, lets talk about something else. We have put some away in here, two bottles of Champagne, two brandy's and two coffees, plus the food, in just over two and a half hours. The bill is just under £1,500, I tip the waiter £50.00, the car costs £250.00 and I tip him £50.00. I have done just under £2,000 by 4.30pm. We arrive back at the hotel and the pair of us pass out on the bed. The next thing I hear is the lavatory flushing, it is dark outside, and Paula comes out of the bathroom. What time is it? Nearly 8pm. I must be going. I cannot thank you enough for such a lovely day. I call her a cab and arrange to meet at Oscars wine bar the following lunch time.

That night I stay in my room feeling dreadful, shaking, sweating, the bed sheets are soaked, the rash has got much worse, it has appeared under my jawline now and I think I am also losing weight. I noticed blood in my urine today, I am very worried but if I go to hospital it is game over.

I meet Paula the next day as arranged. This wine bar is right in the centre of town, I would rather be somewhere a bit more out of sight. I tell her I am staying another week, more business to attend to. It is all done late at night as my clients are overseas, more lies. I even lied about my age, this is just the norm for me now.

What would you like to do today? Well I was thinking of looking for some shoes or a new handbag. Do you fancy Harrods? No, I cannot afford to go there, I was thinking of the high street. I book the same car as before to collect us at 2pm. It is a bit risky but that is what I am all about. I have grown my beard back, dress casual and baseball cap with sunglasses. Paula telephones her mum to tell her where we are going, she is so excited. In one way this makes me feel better knowing that I am in control and calling all the shots

About half way to London, she places her hand on mine. I flinch slightly, but it is a very nice feeling, that someone actually likes me, or likes my money. Then she leans across and kisses me on the cheek, thank you. I am starting to realise after all these years, it is a friend and companion I have been looking for. If and it is a big if, I could settle down with her in a nice cottage in the country, I think I would jump at the chance and leave all this behind me. But deep down I know it is impossible, I am sick of looking over my shoulder every time someone looks at me, my mind goes into overdrive, do I know him? Have I conned him? Is he Police? It may sound like I have everything, but take a look at the big picture, I haven't actually got anything. My mother only tolerates me because I am her son. I know Aunt Ruby wants no more to do with me. So other than Roddy and Paula I am all alone, I know this is of my own doing, I have to live with it. I only bumped into Roddy because I was on the run and Paula, I am sure, only wants my money.

Pulling up outside Harrods she is so excited. I have never been here before. Well, you must enjoy it then. The store is heaving, this panics me to be honest, that is a word I don't use very often. I want to get out of here as soon as possible. I leave her looking at shoes and use the bathroom. I am feeling very faint, there is still blood in my urine, I am struggling, I need to leave as soon as. On my return she is waiting for me, shoes in one hand and a bag in the other. Are you alright? Yes, I just felt a little light headed. So, which do you think, the shoes or the bag? The shoes are £549.00, and the bag is £899.00. Come on let's pay. No, no. It is fine, have both. No, I couldn't. Yes, you can. I pay in cash and call the car back. Why have you bought these for me? Well I have way more money than I need, and I like to treat someone now and then. Thank you, I don't know how to thank you. Well come for dinner with me tonight, come to my room at 7pm. I get the driver to take her home.

I virtually collapse on the bed, utterly exhausted. Before I pass out I will have a look at the web to see what is new. I don't believe this, business man scammed by serial fraudster, some guy is saying he hired me as his office manager and I stole £60,000 from him, he has a solar panel company in Portsmouth. I am furious, I don't mind getting the blame for something I have done, but this is definitely not me. All I can think is there must be another me out there, now that is something to think about, good god.

A siren outside wakes me, it's gone 6.40pm, Paula will be here soon, snort a line and phone down for Champagne and two glasses. It takes me ages to come around, like my batteries have totally run out. My eyes are a bit blood shot and blurry. I neck a brandy from the mini bar and the Champagne arrives, then lay out my clothes on the bed, all designer of course, the labels still attached, I will be wearing over a £1,000 worth tonight. Now Paula is here, I haven't had a shower yet, have some Champagne, I won't be long. Paula looks stunning, I cannot believe some guy let her go, she has her new shoes on and another pair in a carrier bag, these are a bit stiff, so I have got back up. Ok, put some music on, I won't be long.

As I undress, the rash is now all over my lower back, it is spreading like wild fire. I am ready within half an hour and we walk to the Chinese, it is only 10 minutes away. I can see the new shoes are playing her up, but we are here now. I hope you don't mind me saying you look adorable tonight, Paula. You don't look too bad yourself, either. I think we are a good couple, I enjoy her company and I am 90% sure, she enjoys mine.

Into the restaurant, it is busy, it doesn't look anything special but apparently it is the best in town. The meal is excellent, I can always pick fault, but not this time. It has dawned on me, it is not where you are so much as who you are with. She wants to stay in touch when I leave, I know this cannot happen, but I agree all the same. Do you fancy a bar when we leave here? Yes, that would be nice, but I may have to change into my other shoes, these are killing me. Ok, I'm feeling dog rough. Look here's my key, I will sort the bill and meet you back here, I don't think I had it in me to walk back. I pay and focus on finishing the wine, I am fine, sat here, tucked away in the corner. 10 minutes pass, it seems like forever, when you are sat on your own. Then twenty minutes, then thirty, she should have been back by now. I call her, and it goes straight to voicemail. Hello Paula, its me, are you ok, I am still at the Chinese. Five minutes later I try again, nothing. I fear something is wrong.

I walk back, go straight to my room, the door is locked. I try knocking but nothing. Perhaps she has fallen asleep. Reception give me a spare key and I let myself in. My holdall is on the bed, all the cash and the watch are gone. Her old shoes are on the desk with a note reading. Thanks x. I cannot believe I have been done over, £20,000 gone. The bitch, I am livid, every swearword known to man has just left my mouth. I have punched the wall 7 or 8 times. How bloody stupid have I been, I rush down to reception, Sam have you seen Paula? Paula, Yes, the girl I was with earlier. Yes, not long ago, she went upstairs and left by the back entrance. Why, what is wrong? I have to be very careful now, I cannot have Police involved, Oh, nothing, it doesn't matter. Then the manager appears, is there a problem sir? No, I was just looking for Paula, the girl I was with earlier. He takes me to one side, I am sorry to tell you sir, her name is not Paula, it is Kate, she has a reputation across Essex, her speciality is picking up business men in Hotel bars, sleeping with them, then in the morning she has vanished, along with everything of value. Has she stolen from you? No, No, I was just looking for her. She is barred from a lot of hotels and bars around here

I fell flat on my face, she was so lovely, how did I allow this to happen, I even gave her my bloody key. Now back upstairs I have never felt so humiliated, I am a pro, it is me that does this, people just don't get the better of me. I call her time and time again, but I am kidding myself, she is long gone. Someone is at my door, is it her? No, it is Sam from reception, are you ok Sir? Why did no one tell me about her? It is not our business who clients mix with, but you knew what she is like. Management advise us to turn a blind eye, unless something serious happens. I have checked the CCTV and all it shows is her leaving through the back entrance, with a carrier bag. I am lost for words, all I have left is just over £1,000 in my wallet, shit,shit,shit, I thought we were really good together, how bloody wrong can you be. I do know that if the shoe were on the other foot, cannot believe I have said that word and the opportunity arose, I would have done the same.

All I can think is she went through my bags when I was in the shower, maybe it was only jewellery she was after and stumbled across the pot of gold instead. It is a very old trick, women have done this for years, not for one second did I think for once that I would be a victim. All I can do is have a look around the pubs and bars tomorrow, but then I am putting myself at risk, no she is long gone, and I guarantee all she told me was bullshit, for all I know she could live anywhere and be anyone. Just the same as me. This has taught me one important lesson, don't trust anyone and never take your eye off the ball. I am more annoyed with myself than her for being so sloppy and stupid. I am sure the reason we got on so well is because we were the same, so by now she is certainly eyeing up her next victim.

With just over £1,000 left I feel as if I am in the poor house. The way I go on that won't last five minutes. Thank god I have the stash in the loft and the cash coming from mother and George. So, in one way all is not lost. I do want some form of revenge on someone, don't know who yet, but it will make me feel better.

The next morning down for breakfast, I bump into a porter, did she take anything from you sir? No, nothing. Oh, thank goodness, I know I am paranoid, but he showed a lot of interest in what happened. Was this an inside job? Does he tip her off when a rich guest arrives? Something I will never know. I leave my breakfast, I don't think I could hold it down. Back in my room I call mother and let her know I maybe a couple of days, but everything is good, and I have secured the deal. Next call Roddy. Yes, come over, dad is away, it would be great to see you. There is no point in staying around here, I would rather be with Rod. I tell reception I will be leaving tomorrow morning and to book me a taxi for 11 o'clock. I have another little scam in mind.

Chapter 16

I am off to buy a small suitcase and two big bottles of water. That night I pack my belongings into the holdalls and stuff a pillow and the two water bottles into the suitcase. The rest of the night I drink and drink Champagne, wine, vodka, you name it, I have run out of coke now. I am so pissed by 10 o'clock I have wet myself, I cannot even get to the bathroom. Two days ago, I was king of the castle, now the dirty rascal. I am a Sir and demand to be treated as one.

The next morning, I stir, with the stereo still on I try to stand and fall back on the bed. It is ages before I can even focus, to see the time, it is 6.20am and my it stinks in here. I have wet and soiled myself and been sick on the bed, I am mortified, I cannot describe it. I use the bathroom, my face is pure white, red eyes and sweating like a pig. I should clean myself up but first stop a vodka from the mini bar, down in one, I reach but somehow keep it down. I open every window, turn the bedding over and binned my clothes into a holdall, zip it up and leave it in the bath. Now everything is crammed into the two holdalls. I have never in my life been in a state like this. What is happening to me, I am so ashamed. My taxi will be here at 11, so I can try and sort myself out This has been a disaster, but I tell myself it is not the end of the world.

I wait until 11 o'clock and stumble down to reception, my taxi is waiting, I don't even say goodbye, I just want out of here as quick as possible. My driver is Joan, she is very nice and puts my case in the boot and my two holdalls on the back seat. I dread to think what they will think of me when they see the state I have left the room in. I am actually quite ashamed with myself, but onwards and upwards. I tell Joan to stop at Baker Street Station, I need to meet a colleague for 10 minutes, she is fine with that.

Another voicemail from mother asking when I will be back. I call her and tell her that I am delayed in getting the contracts drawn up, but will be with her Tuesday morning, she also tells me the cash is here for me. I am finding her to be a pain in the arse, but there is £70,000 waiting for me, so I can live with that.

We are only 15 minutes from the station, when we pull up I pass her £10.00 and tell her to get herself a coffee and come back in 10 to 15 minutes. Taking my holdalls, but leaving the case in the boot, she drives away. I walk into the station and straight out of the side door into the first cab I see and now I am off to Roddy's. This is a very old trick I have done it many times. I have just saved probably the best part of £100.00, I know she is self employed and has a young family, but I don't care in the slightest, see all it took to lure her was my case in the boot and a

£10 note. Well, at least she will have a case, pillow and two bottles of water. I gave her my number, but that doesn't matter.

Getting near Roddy's I get out two streets away and walk. What a struggle, I am so weak, I can hardly put one foot in front of the other. Finally, I make it, he is waiting for me. God Adam, look at the state of you, you look awful, come in. I collapse into an arm chair and he makes coffee. You should be in hospital. No, no, I have just been burning the candle at both ends that's all. I just need some rest, don't worry. He has stocked up on coke, that is all I am bothered about. I have passed out, I must have drank 10 pints of water, but still feel like shit.

Joan has left a message asking for me to contact her, deleted. That evening we settle for an Indian take away, I am really not up to going out. We settle in the dining room, I cannot eat hardly any of it, I know this ship is sinking fast. After supper we stagger into the sitting room, then out of nowhere. I know who you are, you don't have to lie to me anymore. I am lost for words. What do you mean? I have read all about you on the web, there are even wanted posters in some of the stations. Everybody is looking for you, is it true? Yes, I am not lying to you anymore. My dad forbids me to let you set foot in the house, he would go bloody mad if he knew you were here. Well he is no saint is he. What do you mean? It doesn't matter. Yes, tell me. A quick lie needed, I have heard he is involved in, some less than legit business deals.

I know he has been doing it for years, how long have you been conning people? Do you mind not using that word, I would prefer that I was being economical with the truth, about twenty years. Bloody hell and you have never been caught? That is correct, I am not proud of it, I have done, Lords, Ladies, a politician, business men, you name it I have done them. What on earth made you do it? I explained about being abused in the scouts and my mother moved Gary in after my father died, so I stole £600 and ran off to my Aunts. Which is where I took up with Gwen, she dies after excessive partying and I was on the streets with a £1,000 and a few clothes.

I couldn't go back to my Aunts, I had outstayed my welcome, so it was stay in London or return to Doncaster. How did you survive? I slept with men for money, then started defrauding people. There is no where I have not been, tell a lie, Liverpool, that is probably the only place that has escaped me. What if you get caught? Well, I will just have to face the music I suppose. I take it this is the end of us? No, look I will stick by you, but no more scamming or lying. Yes, I promise, hey that's a word I don't know the meaning of. You can stay until my dad gets back, he will be home Tuesday evening. No worries, I will be gone before that.

Do you want me to make an appointment with my doctor, he is really good? He is in Harley

Street. I am not keen, but on this occasion, I know he is right. My appointment is 10.30am on Monday. I am scared to say the least, but I know I have to go. A taxi to Harley street and I am with Dr Collins in just over an hour. To cut a long story short, he recommends I go straight to hospital, I have Hepatitis, severe liver and kidney damage and very likely heart disease. Oh, and the icing on the cake is, I could have the H.I.V virus as well. I knew it would be bad, but not that bad. I am off to the pub, I need a drink.

That night I explain to Rod, I have high blood pressure and the lack of vitamins, which is almost true. I have lived on coke and booze for the last twenty years. I think he believed me, I am not too sure. I lie awake most of the night, I am well and truly in the shit, a few tablets aren't going to sort this out. Eventually, I sort out my next move. Plant the coke on Ken, get the cash from mothers and disappear abroad. Then seek treatment.

Tuesday morning and I tell Rod I am going to see my mother and I will catch up with him at the weekend, he goes off to work, I know that this is the last I will see of him. I wasn't even man enough to tell him the whole truth, he could have HIV, but the selfish bastard I am, I choose to keep quiet, what a disgrace, I really am.

It is around 11am, Rod has gone, I have just got out of the shower and I can hear someone downstairs. Is that you Rod? I am at the top of the stairs with a towel around me and his dad appears at the bottom. What the hell are you doing here? I popped by to see Rod. Get Out! Get out! Let me get dressed and I will be gone. Oh dear, I really didn't want to bump into him. Dressed I grab my stuff, now downstairs. I told you never to come here again. I know all about you, a two-bit conman. At least I am not a paedophile, he lunges at me and punches me on the right cheek. I fly at him, trading blows, my nose is bleeding, and his face is scratched. Then I try to push him away and he falls backwards, straight through the glass coffee table. Everything falls motionless, like on pause. He is bleeding very badly, I can see a shard of glass sticking out of his neck. Have I killed him? I panic, wash myself off, change my shirt and run. I could have called an ambulance or tried to help him, but no. Look after number 1. I hope he dies slowly, nasty pervert.

A cab to my mothers, she is out. I need to move like yesterday. Another shower, change and next stop the pub. I really have no concern whatsoever for Rods dad, all I am thinking about is myself, as always. This is now pure chaos. My motto of stay calm is not quite working. I have just coughed up a lot of blood, to make matters worse. I grab some cash from the loft and go off to the pub, I feel terrible and look terrible. The sun is out so I have my shades on to cover my eyes.

The pub looks packed. There is even a marque outside. Shit, I don't like this, what is going on? Well, I am here now, no time to turn back, I enter and find a quiet corner. It is a funeral wake; an old villager has passed away. I can only see Ken and a young girl behind the bar. Standing in the corner, shaking like a leaf, Ken approaches, you got the cash? Yes, follow me upstairs in five minutes. Ok, we enter the front bedroom and he gives me a large bag from under the bed. I hand him £2,000, are you sticking about for a bit? Yes, ok, we will have fun later. Well, that is what he thinks. I start to follow him down the stairs and say, I just need the toilet and I will be with you ok. He disappears, perfect, into the bathroom, I wipe my prints off the bag and place it nicely behind the bath panel, job done. Back in the bar, I tell him I will be back tomorrow, when it is quiet. At least somethings gone to plan.

I have got a few hours before mother is home. I have a message on my phone from Sargent Robin Glass, kindly asking me to contact him regarding several urgent matters and it would be in my own interest to do so. Fuck you, you want me, find me. The internet is all covered as well, everybody has seen me or had dealings with me, but still no one has caught me, My loft stash is tucked nicely into my bag, I am just waiting for the other £70,000. I plan to be gone by lunch time at the latest tomorrow,

Tonight, will almost definitely be the last time I see my mother and to tell you the truth I am not bothered at all. It serves her right, putting that asshole Gary before her own children. Hopefully, one day she will realise that. If one day anyone asks me why? I think my answer will be my childhood. Evening comes, and mother is home, all I want is the cash. Oh Adam, you look dreadful. Yes, I had a virus. She asks for the contracts. I am picking them up from my Solicitors in the morning. She is fine with this. She tells me she has the money but cannot hand it over until she has the contracts. Ok, that is fine, no problem. I think I know where the cash is. It is plan B now, it is always good to be one step ahead. Do you have to go to the bank? No, I have it here. Ok, I can guarantee it is under her bed. One thing I am sure of, I know I will find it, more patience required for now, anyway.

We have dinner and settle in for a boring evening in front of the television. Around 8 ish Rod is on the phone hysterical. Calm down, what is wrong? I came home from work and found dad lying on the floor, covered in blood. It looks like he has fallen through the coffee table. Is he alright? He is in St Marys, he has lost so much blood, there is a 70-30 as to whether he will make it. What happened? I don't know, did you see him? No, no, I left not long after you. Perhaps he has had a heart attack or stroke, or maybe just tripped. Was it a break in? No, nothing has been taken. Look, I have to go, the doctors are coming. Ok, look take care, I will call you in the morning. I am not too bothered about his dad, I am more concerned if there is anything linking me to this. Did anyone hear arguing? Did anyone see me leave? If I get done for this I could be facing a possible murder charge, if he dies.

In bed at 10,45pm. I am reminiscing, looking back, my head is all over the place. I must just concentrate on getting the cash and sorting my next destination. I really don't care what happens to anybody else. The thing I am most worried about is my health. It feels like I am shutting down, bit by bit, even my teeth are becoming loose. But first things first.

In the morning I feel dreadful, I can hear mothers alarm going off, it is 6.30am, I know she will be leaving at 8.30am, so I get up. We have coffee and the conversation gets around to when and where I am getting the contracts and what time I will be back. Of course, I make up a nice story and I am certain she has fallen for it. I tell her I will have them by lunch time. Then she wants to know more about the appointment, more bullshit, she seems happy with everything. But my plans are a world away from hers. She goes to get ready for work. Would you like another coffee? Yes please, I won't be long. I have two rohypnol left in my wallet, these will knock her out for a few hours, into her coffee and wait.

It is nearly 7.30am by the time she knows what day it is, I will be on my merry way, seventy grand better off. Perhaps then she will realise what a rubbish mother she really was. Being such a greedy toe rag, I fancy cleaning her out, jewellery box as well. I want her left with nothing, like I was. She is out of the shower and getting dressed. I tap on the door and pass her the coffee. Now I am thinking of hiding places to look first. I know it is not in my room, I have already looked, not to worry I will find it.

Rod has text me, his dad is in a bad way. It doesn't look good and can I call him at some point. Do you know this is me all over, the first thing I thought of is, if he dies, me and Rod could have had everything? I know he has a sister, but I would have conned her out of her share. I think this could be the best one yet. Just fingers crossed he doesn't pull through. Even I think I am the most selfish of people. I am quite shocked at my thinking, but as always put yourself first, think of number one, because no one else will. Just think, the big posh house, money, cars, all for the taking, you seriously couldn't ask for more, but I probably would.

Mother comes back into the sitting room, coffee cup empty and sits in her chair. I feel really tired for some reason. I can see it won't be long now, I am quite excited now, like a little kid going on a treasure hunt. But it is not sweets, it is cash I am after. She is half gone, then, if you hear the door it will be George with my magazine, he picks it up for me, ok mother. I make myself another coffee and wait. I need a shower and get dressed, by the time I return she will be totally zonked out This is also a good time to call crime stoppers and let them know that Ken is dealing and where he keeps his stash. If you ever read this Ken, you will maybe realise you messed with the wrong person. I am sure he will get two years and probably loose the pub as well. Oh, well I will be thinking of him when I am lying on the beach with a cocktail in my hand.

Showered and dressed I am ready for the off, I have terrible stomach ache and I am burning up, still passing blood, this will have to wait, I just want the money. She is fast asleep, I try calling her, but nothing. Right, it is time to search, I will start in her bedroom, I want her left with nothing. First stop empty the jewellery box into my bag, then I hear the door, it is George with her magazine. She is still out of it, I open the door and 3 Police force their way in, Adam Robert Cleaver, I am arresting you for fraud, Shit, it is all over, I am sat down and hand cuffed, I am not saying a word. I look over at mother, she opens her eyes. Do you think you were honestly walking off with £70,000? I saw you put those tablets in my coffee, so I poured it down the sink. I know what you have been up to, it is all over the internet, even newspapers. You were going to rip off George, he is a pensioner, you disgust me. I called the Police when I was in the bathroom. One officer sits next to me and the other two search my room. They have got everything, my phone, my laptop, holdalls, and the loft cash, the lot.

The only thing I said to her, was that I cannot believe that my own mother would turn me in. But knowing what a heartless bitch you are, it doesn't surprise me. I am sorry, but it is for the best, you need help. After about an hour I am taken to Brighton Police station. They are pleased as punch, they finally got me, after all these years. You only caught me because I was grassed up, not because you out smarted me, that shut them up. They couldn't catch a fish, let alone me. I must have passed out, it is nearly midday and we arrive at the station.

Chapter 17

I can hardly stand I am so weak. At the front desk I confirm my name and date of birth. When asked if I have any medical condition, I reel them off, one by one. My clothes and shoes are taken, and I am put in a cell, wearing a white paper suit. I am given some water and told a doctor will be with me shortly. The heat coming off me is like sitting inside a furnace. My nose keeps on trickling blood and my stomach feels like it is going to explode. I am not bothered if I get a massive sentence, I probably won't be around long enough to do it. I know I won't last long, I am damaged beyond repair. A doctor enters my cell, he is with me must be over an hour, he recommends I go straight to hospital, all of my organs are failing, my blood pressure is through the roof. Still hand cuffed, I am taken to Green Park Hospital.

We sit in silence and wait, the devil is waiting for me, I deserve it, the good thing now is that I don't have to look over my shoulder anymore, that is a relief in one way. It may sound odd but for once I can relax. It is very quiet in here, for some reason I am thinking about the abuse I suffered in the Scouts, I wonder if I will bump into any of them in hell? Who knows I may even see Rods dad. We are called in and I do answer all of the questions truthfully, there is nothing to lose now.

Most of my adult life I have had a massive cocaine and alcohol addiction. When I disclosed the intake on an average week the doctor nearly fell over, he doesn't know how I have got this far, he insists that I be admitted, to cut a long story short, he thinks I could die at any minute. I am not scared or frightened at all. What would be better for me, to serve out a long prison sentence, then be dumped into society with no one and nothing, or just fade away being remembered as almost certainly The Best Con Man in Britain. That is an easy decision for me to make, I have my own room number, 3 in Villiars ward. A Police Officer is outside my door, as if I could run off, I am rigged up to machines, and have tubes inserted everywhere.

I keep passing out then coming around again, I am asked if there is anyone I would like to inform, and I decide not. It is nice to be so relaxed and on my own. When I pass out I am back with my nan and brother in happier times and seeing my dad washing his car. I see the neighbours and the plum tree in our garden. I feel myself smiling and trying to say something I don't know what though.

I think I have been lying here for three possible four days now, I am guessing it is Saturday or Sunday. Dr Jeffries has been to see me and asked if I want to be resuscitated if the worst were to happen. I said no thank you. How long do you think I have? Two possibly three weeks, well at least he was straight with me and I thank him for that. I am now incapable of holding a mouth full of water down. Apparently, I am going for a scan later, then I will know exactly what the score is.

I have the scan at 2 o'clock and return to my room, I am given more medication and Linda, one of the nurses looking after me, says, when you were at the scan a reporter from a very well-known tabloid newspaper was here, wanting to know if you wanted to sell your life story. No, it is all I have left, that is the one thing I will be taking with me. Well, if you change your mind, let me know, he left his number. If I were to go ahead with complete honesty, no one would believe it, even I am shocked and embarrassed at some of the activities that led my miserable existence. I must correct myself really wasn't all bad.

The big problem I was facing when Gwen passed away was I was left with nothing, it was do or die, the £1,000 her daughter gave me, it would only last minutes in London and I certainly wasn't ending up in a door way begging, it just wasn't an option. I set out to get what I wanted, I could have stayed in Doncaster and settled for nothing, but I am sure I made the right decision. I wanted better and, in all honesty, I got it. A lot of people in my home town have never even been to London let alone experienced what I did.

Dr Jeffries is back, his face says it all, I am waiting for him to say, do you want the good news or the bad news. I know there is definitely no good news coming my way. Well, here is the bad news, my liver is ruined beyond repair, my kidneys are barely working, oh and I have a tumour on one of them. My heart is struggling to beat, all they can do is keep me as comfortable as they can, until the end. Dr Jeffries says if they attempt to operate, I certainly wouldn't pull through, so it is sit and wait time. Well it is not the first time I have been in a no-win situation, what is the point in worrying now. I know everyone will be glad to see the back of me and I don't blame them.

My lust for money was awful, I would have taken your child's pocket money, I didn't care whatsoever as long as I had it, how dreadful, but what's done is done. I cannot turn the clock back. The world was my oyster.

That evening, two different nurses are with me, my eyesight is also fading now, I can barely see them. I couldn't argue if I wanted to. How different is this, other people telling me what is happening, I always called the shots, but not anymore. Somehow, I made it through the night, I am not sure what they are giving me, but I am seeing spiders, fire, even people I hated, they have all come back to see me, even the kids that bullied me in Primary School. Even from day one no one liked me it was as if, one in a 100 is a total misfit, for some reason I was the chosen one.

I am now in the hospice, you can smell death, it has got a certain odour, I can't explain it. I am just lying here now, as far as I am aware no one has visited me, but I wouldn't know anyway. Thinking about it, the only people that liked me were the ones who wanted something, but it always backfired on them.

Another thing that bugs me is why people are so frightened of death. It is the best I have felt for a long time, the burden has been lifted, I am floating and fully relaxed, it is not a problem anymore. I spent most of my life running and hiding, now it is all over, what a lovely feeling. There is only one person I would love to see one last time, that is Roddy. More than anything just to say sorry and I loved him. What a truly lovely guy, I regret not meeting him years ago, I am certain we would have gone places, maybe even got married and settled down, but it is all too late now.

I have no idea what day or time it is, I am feeling very cold and shivery, I cannot speak or see now. I have just enough strength to raise my left hand as a thank you gesture, it is the only thing that is left. Some questions I am sure need to be answered, I will be as truthful as I can, I am not lying, I will answer the best I can.

Do you have any regrets? Yes, I should have looked after myself better and quit while I was ahead.

What would you have done if you hadn't done this? I am not too sure, maybe worked for a charity, to help other people who had been abused.

Would you have done anything different? Yes, definitely, first of all stayed away from drugs and London. Kept in touch with Robert and do my hardest to find Roddy?

Why did you do it? I didn't want to spend my whole life with nothing. Being poor, I witnessed my parents and grandparents have it, but it wasn't for me.

Do you feel any kind of remorse? No not at all, if people will be so stupid and gullible, what do they expect. At the end of the day I was just an actor with a silly posh accent and everyone fell for it. Everybody lies whether it is to get a girlfriend/boyfriend, a bank loan or mortgage. I was just the same but on a much higher scale.

So where are they now?

Well, this is as far as I am aware, the dealers are still looking for me, as are the chauffer's and taxi drivers, good luck to them.

The solicitor I ripped off for £20,000, has now retired, he still has his love for cocaine and young men, his wife knows but chooses to ignore it.

Jay is currently serving life for stabbing another dealer to death. Apparently, it was a meet that went very wrong.

Stuart is still at the hotel; he and his wife are still trying to come to terms with what I did to them.

All I know about the Oxford boys is that they both got kicked out of university and are still squandering their parent's money.

Kate the girl who ripped me off in Essex has turned over a new leaf, she lives with her boyfriend in Bristol and works as a secretary, she is also four months pregnant, I wonder if it is a boy, she could name him after me.

Ken the slimy bastard got two years three months for possession with intent to supply. Also, money laundering. His wife has left him, and The Grapes is up for sale.

Roddy's dad made a full recovery, that is a shame, all he has said is that he had a funny turn, which caused him to fall. His abuse still remains a secret to this day.

Roddy has remained single and given up drink and drugs. I think he needs some quiet time after being with me.

George still lives in his flat, counting his lucky stars he didn't lose his life savings.

Aunt Ruby has now fully retired and does charity work one day a week. She denies all knowledge of ever knowing me.

Pete who I lodged with, got married and emigrated to Canada, he has two children and is doing well.

Finally, my mother, yes, my wonderful mother, she is thinking of selling up and moving to Portugal. The embarrassment is too much for her to handle. I dare say she will land on her feet.

Oh, I nearly forgot Lady Penelope, I have definitely changed her perspective of people, she trusts no one and stepped down from her role in the charity. A couple of weeks after the auction, she gave £30,000 of her own money to cover what I stole.

If you take time to read this, please do not copy me. You are only here once, enjoy it and make the most of it. You only get one chance, for me I was doomed from the start. A car crash waiting to happen. I was a misfit, damaged goods that no one wanted. I chose the route I travelled, I only have myself to blame and was it worth it? No, I don't think so.

I just want to go now, I was never one for hanging around, I know it is nearly time to move on. I wonder what is on the other side, perhaps another journey, I just hope it is a better one. If I had a receipt for my life I would take it back.

I passed away in my sleep at 3.22am on the 10th May 2017, eight days after my birthday, I was 37, with a nurse holding my hand. They were so nice to me, I cannot thank them enough. Perhaps, they didn't know who I was.

My funeral is scheduled for 11am on the 19th, I am being cremated, I will be interested to see who shows up. With a tag on my left ankle and bagged up, I am a terrible mess. I really did destroy myself, my hair has virtually gone, my teeth have fallen out, I am a nasty shade of greeny yellow, blind and I weigh just over 5 stone.

It is the morning of the 19th and show time. The only people here are the undertakers and a couple of staff from the hospice. The only flowers I have are two red roses on top of my coffin, reading love always Rod x. My ashes are buried in the garden of the hospice, with a small wooden cross by the side. On my death certificate my cause of death was acute liver failure. It was slightly disappointing to see no one attended my funeral, not even my own mother, but I am not surprised, she was a selfish cow, that is probably where I inherited it from.

All that remains left to say is never trust anyone, especially a posh, well dressed, Sir, that appears from nowhere. Oh, just one last thing, I never did get to 50. I am very similar to god in many ways, I have many followers, everyone wants to be with me, they will do anything for me and give me everything, but no one can find me.

THE END

This book is based on a real person, names, places and events have been changed. Some events have been made up.

I would like to dedicate this, my first book to my wife Joan and daughters Kate and Anna. Also, my very dear friend Mr Martin Andrew Cottle, whom sadly is no longer with us, and his family, all of which have been a huge tower of strength and a massive inspiration throughout my life. I thank you all.

Lots of Love
Jon

Martin Andrew Cottle
3rd June 1962- 6th November 2016